THE SHEEP WALKER'S DAUGHTER

Sydney Avey

Basque Originals

THE SHEEP WALKER'S DAUGHTER

Sydney Avey

Center for Basque Studies
University of Nevada, Reno

This book was published with the generous financial support of the Basque government.

The Center for Basque Studies
University of Nevada, Reno
www.basque.unr.edu

Library of Congress Control Number: 2017954869

For California's Valley of the Heart's Delight, nurturer of dreams, and the Central Valley, one of the world's most productive agriculture regions, and for my tribe: Nellie Belle, Opal, Shirley, Cheryl, April and Audrey.

Part 1

LOSING LEORA

❧ Dolores ❧

1

INTRUDERS

September 1953

I stand at the bedroom door while the coroner examines the corpse. He lifts the sheet to cover Leora's face. I had not thought to do that. Does this guard her dignity? Shield her from prying eyes? Or does this protect the living from witnessing the horror of death, the emptiness of a once-cherished body now void of a soul? Not that I ever cherished Leora, or she me. *I hate this whole mess.* But now is not the time to have such uncharitable thoughts.

Leora seemed to leave life one body part at a time. Cataracts formed over her eyes and she could no longer read her magazine stories. Her ears became attuned to only high notes; Saturday evening's *Your Hit Parade* annoyed her.

"Turn that mess off," she would grumble at me.

Her joints seized up and easy movement became a memory. Then memory itself became irretrievable. Her heart forgot how to beat, and so she died.

I follow the coroner into the kitchen and watch him spread his paperwork out on the kitchen table.

Carbon copies flutter in the predawn breeze that slips in through the window I forgot to close last night. I stumble over the simplest answers to his requests for information for the death certificate.

When my husband died, he was sitting at his metal desk in Korea. We had made it through World War II even though, like all Army wives, I was prepared to receive bad news. I would do so with grace and decorum, tears and resolve, I believed. But Henry survived that war and I let my guard down.

Then three years ago, an Army officer, shiny brass leaves sparkling on the shoulders of his dress uniform, surprised me on a Saturday morning in my vegetable garden. I was plucking brittle squash vines from their final resting place on the hard clay dirt that I fight with every growing season. Lieutenant Colonel Henry James Carter had gone overseas again, but I had decided not to stay in the housing at the Presidio. Instead, I gave up my job at the bank and left San Francisco to care for my ailing mother in the small Craftsman cottage in Los Altos that Henry and I had bought for her. My fingers had just curled around a crookneck squash, a straggler in what had been a surprisingly good harvest, when the crunch of tires on the gravel driveway interrupted my gardening.

I was certain that Henry would come home from Korea. But he didn't. His commanding officer found him slumped over his desk, dead of a massive heart attack.

As I received this news, I stood in my garden holding the squash and watching the soldier's mouth move while the whole Pacific Ocean roared in my ears. Leora had every bit of her hearing then. Leaning on her cane in the front doorway, she took in his words and then shuffled back inside the house to her bedroom and shut the door.

I tried to pay attention to the soldier's words: Did I want to go inside and sit down? Did I want him to call someone? Did I understand I would receive a call in a few days about the arrangements to transport Henry's body back to the States? Would I be sure to fill out the paperwork that guaranteed me survivor benefits? Could he get me a glass of water?

I stood there in the dirt, the sun of a California Indian summer burning into my shoulders. I pictured Henry in his colorless world across a gray ocean, dead on a gray desk in a gray country governed by a sea of gray men in gray uniforms. Then I doubled over and threw up.

The soldier took a handkerchief from his pants pocket and handed it to me. We walked into the house. I went to the kitchen and poured us each a glass of water.

"Ma'am," he said, as I handed him his water, "I can't leave until you have someone here with you." We both looked toward the closed bedroom door. I moved to the telephone table.

"I will call my daughter. She's at Stanford. She can be here in thirty minutes."

I dialed Valerie's phone number and when he was sure that someone had answered the phone, the soldier looked around for a place to set down the envelope he had in his hand. I held out my hand to take it and then turned my back to him. He left.

Things are different this time. I won't call Valerie yet.

The coroner leaves and I enter Leora's bedroom one last time. I pull the sheet off her face and study her in the morning light that is beginning to flash through the branches of the pepper tree near the window. The sun snaking up the back of that tree surprises me with its early intensity and brings tears to my bleary eyes.

The glow of my mother's well-cared-for skin has cooled to form the waxy gray mask of death. I replay her struggle over the past year in my head, trying to understand the interplay between a body losing control and a mind holding on to secrets—secrets that my mother has taken with her to the grave.

There is something else I must do. I pull a stool out of the closet and go to the window. On top of the stool, I struggle to loosen the window frame from its casement until it opens. This takes all the energy I have left, but now Leora's soul can depart. That was one of the few traditions my mother taught me.

I climb down from the stool, stiffness knotting my shoulders and settling in my lower back. I fall back down on the kitchen chair I had pulled into Leora's room earlier in the week. I'm sitting there, trying to stretch out my spine, when the sound of leather-soled shoes slap, slap, slapping up the gravel driveway and the three red cement porch steps precedes two sharp thumps on the green doorjamb. David from the mortuary is here already. He must not have wanted to drive his hearse down the narrow driveway and risk scratching his doors on the hedge I have been meaning to trim. That means a trip down the driveway into the road on a gurney for Leora, in full view of the neighbors.

It isn't long before voices out by the mailbox signal that my neighbors are beginning to gather like a crowd of chattering crows. They keep a respectful distance from the hearse and I hide behind the screen door. David apologizes, assuring me that he can handle the transfer discreetly. After the hearse rolls away, the conversation continues and the neighbors elect an emissary to come to the door. If I had any sense, I would go out and get it over with, but good sense seems to have departed along with Leora.

They choose old Mrs. Dold, who rarely leaves her house these days. She limps up my driveway on swollen feet. I open the screen door and come out onto the porch to save her the effort of climbing the steps.

"Dolores, I'm so sorry about your mother." She looks up at me, her watery blue eyes locking on to mine.

"Thank you, Mrs. Dold. She didn't suffer. She went in her sleep."

She leans on her cane at the bottom of the steps. She wants to know if I need anything. She wants to know about the funeral service. She wants to know if she can call her pastor to help me through this difficult time. No, no, no, I tell her gently. She was a good friend to my mother, a woman who didn't have many friends.

The crows have flown. With my last ounce of energy, I strip the bed that Leora died in, intending to take the sheets to the garage and wash them. Instead, I sit back down on the kitchen chair by the bed and contemplate the little altar of memorabilia Leora had arranged on her nightstand when she knew she was going to die. I try to get inside her head, always an impossible feat for me. Why did she choose these particular mementos for comfort?

I pick up a cheap picture frame and catch my fingertip on the corner where the metal edges don't meet. The cut is deep and painful. I pop my finger in my mouth, pin two flaps of sliced skin together with my teeth, and probe the wound with the tip of my tongue, sucking metallic-tasting blood into my mouth. My finger throbs clear to my sit bones. I try to focus on the glossy black-and-white photo housed in the frame.

Two delighted faces shine out at me. A triumphant Leora sports a black feathered hat with a saucy veil. She fluffs her stylish bob with one hand. Her other hand rests on the shoulder of a young girl—Valerie when she was about eight years old. Valerie's dimpled chin perches on her chubby little fist. Her dark eyes gaze out in the same direction as her grandmother's. They are admiring themselves in a mirror.

I remove my finger from my mouth and reach for the rosary beads spilled on the table. I never knew Leora to be particularly religious. I set them back down and reach across the dusty maple nightstand to pick up a bell. It lays heavy in my hand, a cast-iron relic coated in brass and missing the clapper. It looks like a cowbell, only smaller. I roll it over and discover an inscription in a language I can't identify—*Ardi galdua atzeman daiteke, aldi galdua berriz ez.* Then that unwelcome crunch of tires grates on the gravel again.

Pain returns to my spine and shoulders. The screen door pops open, squeaking in protest, and a sharp, insistent rapping rattles the front door.

The heavy breathing of a large man who doesn't handle stairs well is the tipoff. If I am very quiet, maybe he will go away. He doesn't. I curl my fingers around the bell. This call is not unexpected. I go to the door and open it.

"Mr. Belch."

"It's Beche." He curls his lip into a poor excuse for a smile. "I'm here to collect the money your mother owes me. Where is she?" He has put his foot over the threshold as if he is expecting me to slam the door in his face. He is so close that I am overpowered by the odor of his Old Spice losing the battle under his armpits.

"She's dead," I hiss.

"Nice try." His smile broadens and he yells over my shoulder. "Mrs. Moraga, it's no use siccing your daughter on me. You are ninety days overdue and you need to pay up."

He has lugged his black sales case full of brushes up the steps. He's hoping that if he collects his due from Leora, he can sell her more useless cleaning implements. What I've been able to tolerate in the past, the game these two have played over how much crap he can talk her into and how long she can put off paying the bill, ignites a choking fury deep in my chest. I puff up like a cobra, gather as much height as I can, and I strike, pushing the big man so hard in the chest that he is jettisoned off the landing. He tries to keep his balance by grabbing for the railing. I am cocking my arm, rage burning in my eyes, so he grabs his case and hightails it for his car. I fling the bell as hard as I can at his head, missing him and denting the driver's door instead. He is turning the ignition before his behind hits the seat, gunning the car in reverse, spraying gravel everywhere. The hedge brambles claw the paint off his Nash Rambler. My mailbox splinters as he backs into it and then gears forward to make his escape.

I could not have shed enough tears in a lifetime to feel the release I am experiencing now. Searching the ground for my bell, my pounding heart begins to find its rhythm, my breathing settles down, and a deep, warm chuckle that is not my own fills my ears. I look up to see a priest standing before me.

❦ Dolores ❧

2

BRASS URNS

*A*pie-faced man stands in my driveway. He erupts with the warm, hearty laugh of a man who is truly tickled. The humor of the situation finally strikes me and I laugh too. Big, gulping guffaws burst out from the same place that breathed smoke and fire an instant ago. I laugh until I hurt.

The priest stoops to retrieve my brass missile, walks up the steps with me, places the bell in my hand, and then covers it and my hand with his own. He shakes my hand so hard that the gravel lodged inside the bell rattles like a maraca.

"I'm Father Mike. Mrs. Dold sent me."

"Oh, she shouldn't have done that." I pull my hand away. The sun is beginning to disappear behind the pepper tree that shades the front door and a chill sets in. It's easier to invite him in than to think about how to make him go away.

He's a modest-sized man for someone with such a big head. He follows me into the kitchen. Although speaking to the clergy is not on my list of favorite things to do, he is more welcome than the parade that has passed through my day so far. I want to make him laugh again, but I can't think how. I strike a match and light the burner on the stove to heat water for tea.

"Dolores, I'm very sorry for your loss. It's not been a very happy birthday for you, has it?"

"Mrs. Dold told you that?"

"Your mother told me that. She told me you were born on September fifteenth, the Feast Day of the Seven Sorrows of Mary."

Stinging, bitter tears spring from my eyes. Five different retorts spin in my head like balls whirling in a roulette wheel. I opt for the most accessible one when the wheel slows down.

"You knew my mother, then?"

"Oh, yes. She came to church with Mrs. Dold. You didn't know that?"

"Well, I knew she walked over to Mrs. Dold's every Sunday morning, but I didn't know they went anywhere. Frankly, I'm surprised. Forgive me, Father, but my mother hated Catholics."

He grins like a Cheshire cat, his eyes peering at me over mounds of cheekbones. "I should have explained. I am not a Catholic priest. I'm the rector at Saint Matthew's. It's an Anglican church—similar traditions, different governance, no pope."

"And you knew my mother well enough that she talked to you about me?" I reach for a canister of tea bags, plop the chamomile one he asks for into a mug, and drown it in boiling water. Then I pour the rest of the water over the English Breakfast tea bag I've chosen for myself. I slide his mug across the table and sit down at the other end.

Father Mike sits up straight, arranging his face to conceal the humor that seems to be a natural part of his complexion. "She talked a lot about you, Dolores."

"Actually, I go by Dee. I wasn't pleased when I discovered I'd been named for the patron saint of sadness."

"I understand. Well, Dee, um . . . " Father Mike obviously has something on his mind. But I'm in no mood to make it easy for him. "Are you aware of what your mother's wishes were regarding her final resting place?"

"No. I'm not aware she had any wishes about . . . that." My plan is to meet with David at Spangler's Mortuary in a day or so and let him walk me through whatever is necessary. Leora didn't leave a will. Apparently, though, she had confided in this stranger.

Our conversation is interrupted by the series of short rings that signal a phone call for me and not my neighbor who shares the phone line. I've always found the term *party line* to be offensive. If it's my call, I don't want anyone else to be a party to it. But there it is. I have developed the habit of monitoring my words for the effect they might have when they are passed around with a plate of doughnuts at the morning coffee hour next door.

"Excuse me, I need to get this." I disappear behind the doorframe, lift the telephone receiver from its cradle, and brace my shoulder against the wall.

It's my boss, Mr. Bradley. He inquires after my mother's health with all the interest of a grocery-store clerk handing me my S&H Green Stamps while measuring the contents of the next customer's cart to see how many bags he'll need. "Do you think you can make it into work next week? The invoices are really piling up on your desk."

My desk at General Electric Company; I'd like to be sitting there right now. Pencils sharpened and ready to go, my typewriter square in front of me, a fresh notepad to my left, my adding machine to the right, my in-box in the corner, nothing else. My heart races like a ground squirrel that has just spotted his hole and dashed for cover. My desk is not safe, though. Mr. Bradley is a beady-eyed bird of prey circling high above, watching for one member of the colony to make a mistake. It was my mistake to take the last week of Leora's life off work, because now I'm going to have to ask for more time.

"Actually, Mr. Bradley, my mother died this morning." I pick a pencil up off the telephone table and drum it on the message pad. "I'm going to need a little more time off to make arrangements."

"Dee." His voice drips with disappointment, but it's not for me or my dead mother. "I'm sorry for your loss. Take tomorrow off. I need you back in the office on Monday. I don't know if I can hold your job past that."

"Mr. Bradley, you know I'm entitled to three days of compassion leave." He will probably have to look that word up in the dictionary. I doodle with the pencil while he does some heavy sighing.

"You've had a week, Dee."

"I took vacation, Mr. Bradley, to take care of my sick mother. Now I have to bury her. Don't you have a mother, Mr. Bradley?" I've gone too far. I explain that the invoices don't have to be paid until the end of the month and offer to return to work early next week and work late to make up the time.

"You know I can't pay overtime, Dee." I snap the pencil in two with one hand.

"I'll take the work home. You won't have to pay me overtime."

"Okay, Dee." His voice warms like a snake that has felt the morning sun. "Let us know if you need anything." Click. He's gone.

I pivot around the doorframe back into the kitchen and glare at Father Mike.

"Okay, what does she want?"

My jaw drops at what he tells me. My mother has purchased three spaces in a columbarium on a wall inside a chapel on the grounds of Saint Matthew's. She wants to be walled up! This is like something out of Edgar Allan Poe. I have to ask Father Mike what a columbarium is. He explains the process of cremation and interment. There are different kinds of crypts, but apparently Leora wanted to be on display because she purchased three elaborate brass urns that will be visible behind glass. Before he leaves, Father Mike shows me a picture.

"Why three?" I ask.

He shrugs and looks away. Did she intend for Valerie and me to stand with her in eternity behind glass? How very like her, to assume that Valerie will never marry and that I won't be buried beside Henry at Golden Gate Cemetery, the burial ground for war veterans. Now that I think of it, I'm not sure I ever actually made those arrangements.

Father Mike has instructed me to think about how I want to honor my mother. She will be cremated, and interment can happen anytime. I have mixed emotions about Father Mike. His intrusion and his allusions to an intimacy with my mother that I didn't know she was capable of irritate my stomach. On the other hand, he has cleared a path in one short visit that will allow me to move forward. Somehow, the thought of Leora shelved like a treasured book in a library of souls comforts me. Tears flood my eyes. I've never thought of my mother as a treasure.

Treasure. I roll that word around on my tongue. Leora was not one who cared a lot about possessions, but she did have her treasures. The fog that rolls in from the ocean near Santa Cruz has cooled the air that sifts into the front room through the screen door, a moist chill that prompts me to begin closing up the house. I turn on the lights and go on a hunt for my mother's treasures.

Midnight finds me sitting on the pitted wood floor surrounded by relics I have pulled from drawers—trinkets I found in the pockets of Leora's old sweaters, memorabilia I have retrieved from the steamer trunk in the back of the garage, and souvenirs I have discovered in a valise she kept under her bed. Among the objects that stare at me are a bright yellow gargoyle with incense-stained teeth that smells of sandalwood, a bronze bust of an enigmatic young woman with the curl of a smile forming on her lips, and a shiny teal goose with a graceful curve to its neck. As I finger the costume jewelry I've piled on the floor, I contemplate these things I've seen before—but not ever really *seen*. They tell a story I've never asked to hear.

I can't keep all this stuff. The sad fact is no one wants any of it. Valerie is a gypsy, moving around the world with her life packed in a duffle bag. Most likely, she'll give up her apartment in Palo Alto when she's done with school and return to Spain, the country she fell in love with on a foreign exchange program. Then I will be finally, irrefutably alone. How did it come to be that Valerie and I are at the end of a line that pulled apart like fragile yarn tugged too hard from a tight ball of wool?

An aftershock of grief roars up from a deep place. I lie on the floor, rolling my head slowly back and forth on the waxy wood to relieve the pressure in my temples. What am I crying about? The trinkets on the floor? No, I'm mourning the family I never had. Surely there are people somewhere I never knew and will never know. Why did I stop asking Leora about who we were, where we came from? Because I knew she wouldn't tell me the truth.

Valerie isn't telling what she knows either.

❧ Valerie ❧

3

TANGLED WEBS

*M*y novel is going to be published in Spain. Professor Warner found me in the library stacks and said, "Miss Carter, I've received word that Mondadori is going to take your book." My stomach did flip-flops. Flip, I'm an author. Flop, I can't let my mother know about this. How did I let things get this far?

Only two people know how this book came to be: Professor Warner and Wallace Stegner, the head of the Stanford Creative Writing Program. Even though my story flowed easily onto paper after a chance remark Professor Stegner made in a seminar, it has never been easy for me to acknowledge the truth. I teased this story out of my grandmother and never told my mother that she may have a sister.

Professor Stegner had told his class of fledgling novelists that we should create our own personal histories. "You may not know who you are, or who your character is, but you know where you came from. Write about that, and you will discover who you are, who your character is."

The thing is, I don't know where I came from. Not exactly, but I've guessed at some of it and made up the rest. Leora gave me clues, but my mother can't know that. Mom must not know that I managed to wrest information from my tight-lipped grandmother that she refused to tell her own daughter. I will not be the one to tell my mother that although she was raised as an only child, there might have been another one. If it's true, Leora should have told her. That's my only irritation with Leora though, because she was always so generous with me. She said we were kindred spirits. Strong women.

I've let Mom go on thinking I'm still writing a scholarly account of the influence of the Spanish Civil War on Spanish literature. But the truth is that I set my thesis aside more than a year ago when I started writing an historical novel based on imagining our family history. It's about two sisters separated during the Spanish Civil War, when many Basque children were evacuated to Eastern and Western Europe. One sister returns to Spain with her father after the war. The other sister gets caught in Russia with her mother and eventually ends up in the United States.

Whenever I try to talk to my mother about where we came from, she gets mad. Writing my story in Spanish and publishing it in Spain means I won't have to explain my interest in a family history she doesn't give a fig about. I have this all planned out. I will take a semester in Spain, get back to writing my thesis, and work with the publisher of my novel to get it to press. I will dedicate my book to *mi abuela*, Leora Moraga.

I'm in such a state as I walk through the quad that my shoulder slams into the bulging book bag of an undergrad. I stumble and he gives me the bleary-eyed look of a biology major that has been looking at Petri dishes under a lab light for too long. He mumbles an apology even though it's my fault. Leora always told me I can't walk a straight line to save my life, and it's true.

I stop and look up. I've been walking toward Mem-Chu. Whenever life hands me a perfect moment, I come here to let the graceful Spanish architecture of Stanford Memorial Church give me a benediction. I gaze up at the cross that stands in noon relief against a cloudless expanse of bright blue sky. As the bells chime their midday greeting, I say a quick prayer. Then I veer off to the bike racks, hop onto my Silverlight racer, and speed off to meet Peter for a late lunch.

Riding my bike invigorates me. My knees bounce the petticoat underneath my favorite circle skirt, swishing it from side to side as I pump across El Camino toward Emerson Street. My ponytail whips across my cheek in the fall wind and my eyes tear from the cold, or maybe it's the pollen in the air. I slow to a stop in front of the Peninsula Creamery and lock my bike up next to Peter's. My heart flip-flops when I spot Peter through the window. He is sitting at our table, drinking a Coke and talking to a couple of girls who don't seem in too much of a hurry to find their own table. I slow down and busy myself looking at the jawbreakers in the gumball machine. I spot a blue one and the inside of my mouth moistens. When I look up again, the girls have moved back to their own booth.

I shouldn't do this, but I swing my hips slightly as I walk toward Peter. Coming up behind him, I run a finger along the back of his neck and tease it across his closely clipped hair a couple of times. He turns to me and a slow, crooked smile breaks across his face, but it's his eyes that undo me. Deep set and sparkly blue, half shaded by blond-tipped curly brown lashes, his eyes catch the light and invite me in.

"Hello, baby," he says in the practiced way that always reminds me that Peter is a man who knows the effect he has on women. He pats the bench next to him and I drop in.

"Guess what, Peter?"

He raises a finger and signals to the waitress to bring me a Coke. Then he shifts his body to face me and says in all seriousness, "I'm all ears."

Then he wiggles his ears. "How *do* you do that?"

"But we digress. What's your news?" He rests his rugged jaw on his hand.

"I just got the word. My book is going to be published in Spain."

"That's great, Val." Peter hunches over his Coke. He uses his straw like an Electrolux to suck the last of his soda pop from the melting ice at the bottom of the glass while making googly eyes at me. I look at him without appreciation. He straightens up.

"Really, Val. That's great. Does this mean you will have to go to Spain?"

"Well, I don't have to, but I want to."

"You know, cookie, you've never told me what this book of yours is about." He loops an arm around me and scoots me over closer to him on the bench. Lowering his voice, he taps his ear. "I know it's some sort of a secret, but you can tell old Pete. Just whisper it here, in old Peter's ear."

I have to think about this. People are going to ask what the book is about. I whisper in Peter's ear. "I will, but not now."

I explain that I have to get going so I can tidy up my apartment before my study group meets. We finish our hamburgers and fries, share a couple of long kisses by the bike rack, and then bicycle back to campus. He heads off for baseball practice and I weave my bike through the late afternoon student traffic, playing a scene in my head. Like the professors who entertain students in their elegant College Avenue homes, I will fix some ice tea and cookies to serve to my study group, and then I'll share my news. I'm wiggling the key in my door lock when the phone starts ringing inside.

It was a short conversation. At the same moment that tears sting my eyes, fingers of fury tighten around my heart. How could my mother not tell me!

"I'm telling you now," she said.

"Was she sick?" I'm trying to make sense of this sudden void in my life.

Leora is dead. *Mi abuela está muerto.* Lita is dead. If I say it enough times, in enough different ways, maybe I will believe it. My Lita is dead; I wasn't there; she was sick for months; I didn't know; no one told me. My mother waited two days to call me. Why? Well, why should that surprise me? After all, my mother pretty much stopped talking to me the day she learned that my father had died overseas.

I didn't know my father very well. He was a war hero, but I remember him mostly for the treats and trinkets he brought home from foreign countries: chocolates from Belgium, tiny wooden shoes from Holland, flowery perfume from France. He was posted to various Army headquarters most of my life. We didn't go with him because my mother preferred to stay in officers' quarters at the Presidio. She didn't talk much about him when he was away. I had just returned from my year in Spain and was finishing up my undergraduate work when my father died. My mother went into her shell after that. It made me uncomfortable and I stopped going home.

Home was never much of a place for us Carters and Moragas. My mother grew up living in hotel rooms with Leora because my grandmother traveled for her job. Mom went to high school in Portland, Oregon, and art school in Los Angeles, where she met an air corps recruit named Henry Carter and married him. That's all I know about my mother's life.

I remember the military housing we lived in, but when I think of home, I think of the cozy bungalow on Lundy Lane in Los Altos even though I never actually lived there. I visited Leora a lot before my mother moved there from the city, after my father went to Korea. Leora and I would sit at the kitchen table by the window and play canasta, or pull the chairs into the living room where the TV was and watch *Kraft Television Theatre*. I asked her once why her living room had only a piano in one corner, a TV set in another, and a telephone table just outside the door to the kitchen. She explained that she only ever had a bedroom, a bathroom, and a kitchenette when she was working and living in hotels. She didn't know how to furnish a living room and didn't really need one, she said. When neighbors came to visit, she stood at the screen door for hours and talked to them. But she never invited them in. She didn't play the piano either.

Thinking about all this has calmed me down a little, but I can't deal with my study group this afternoon.

I go into my bedroom and pack some clothes. On my way out, I scribble a sign and tack it to the front door:

STUDY GROUP CANCELED. DEATH IN THE FAMILY. BACK NEXT WEEK.

❧ Dolores ❧

4

THE HOUSE THAT JACK BUILT

Valerie bangs into the front room and drops her duffle bag on the floor while I'm talking on the phone. I point her toward the bedroom and slip around the doorframe into the kitchen where I can continue my conversation in private.

"Excuse me, Roger, Valerie just got here. What were you saying?"

"Dee, I hope I'm not interrupting your time with your family. I wanted to call and make sure you're alright. I just heard that your mother passed. I'm so sorry."

Roger is the controller at General Electric and the head of my department. Unlike Mr. Bradley, he is patient, kind, and understanding. He's all business too, but he is the kind of man you can relax and be yourself with. I like him.

"Don Bradley is an asshole, Dee. I know I shouldn't say that, but don't let him bully you into coming back before you're ready. Your job will be here. We really can't operate without you."

"It's nice to know you feel that way, Roger."

"Do you have plans for a funeral service? I . . . the department would like to send flowers."

"We'll be doing a private interment at Saint Matthew's. I'll let you know." I look up to see Valerie standing in the doorway. "I need to go Roger, thank you so much for calling. I'll see you next week." I hang up the phone.

"It's nice to know you feel that way, Roger." Valerie mimics me. "How exactly does Roger feel? And who is Roger?"

Valerie has a flair for drama and a nose for a story. She's not being mean, she's being Valerie. But I'm not in the mood. I explain that Roger is my supervisor and that he is feeling concerned, unlike the big boss, Mr. Bradley, who is feeling put out because I've taken time off.

"That's awful." She wrinkles her nose. "What's all that stuff on the floor?" She surveys the altar of Leora's memorabilia arranged like a miniature Stonehenge, a mute testimony to an unknown past.

"It's all stuff that belonged to your grandmother." I'm suddenly finding it hard to talk about Leora in the past tense. "If there is anything there that you want . . . " I picture her stuffing the teal goose into her duffle bag and think better of my offer, "I can store it for you for when . . . " I don't know how to finish that sentence. When you finish your degree? When you get a real job? When you get married? Anything I say will get me in trouble.

"It's okay, Mother, there isn't anything I want except maybe some photographs."

"We can go through them." "Not now."

And now we are at the end of our words. Valerie walks out on the service porch, through the back door and down the steps. I follow her, taking a moment to look at the cardboard box made into a bed that gave warmth to so many of Leora's little dogs. Posie, her black-and-white cocker spaniel; Scoshie, the dachshund and Chihuahua mix; Roxie, the miniature greyhound— they all lived into old age. I can't walk through here without seeing them thumping their tails on their beds, pulling themselves up out of warm blankets to walk stiff- legged over to the dog dish Leora refreshed on the hour to keep them interested in their food. I picture them frolicking somewhere, glad to have her attention again.

I walk out into the yard and down the pink stepping stones shaped like playing-card suits—hearts and diamonds, spades and clubs. Valerie is leaning on the short fence that marks the end of our property.

I love the quiet moments I've spent looking down into the creek bed, watching the water burble over the smooth rocks. Willow trees lean into the water and trail their branches like children swirling their fingers in the soft eddies. Dragonflies dart and zoom, circle and skate. A radio plays in the distance from somewhere across the creek.

Valerie looks up and her pretty brown eyes widen and spill over with tears. "I should have been here with you. I should have been here with Lita." Her voice rises to a shrill pitch. "Why didn't you tell me?" Then she erupts like a pent-up geyser. "Why don't you ever talk to me?"

Valerie's face is a kaleidoscope of change: red anger becoming white despair, becoming purple outrage, becoming pink shame and disappointment—a blur of colors that scorch her creamy Mediterranean skin.

My face goes pale. The oxygen rushes from my
lungs. *Why the hell does she use Spanish to refer to Leora? Leora was Greek, for God's sake.* I say nothing. To
my credit, I squirm a bit with shame at her accusation
about our poor communication. But I will not cry at
my daughter's bidding. I've cried enough. We look at
each other and I burst into tears.

"I'm sorry, Mom," she says. She hasn't called me
that in years. I'm really sick of the frosty *Mother.*

"It's okay, honey." I put my arm around her and
we walk back up to the house.

We drive to Saint Matthew's to meet with Father
Mike about the interment and memorial service he
has proposed. I take comfort in discovering that Valerie is just as surprised as I was to learn of Leora's
wish to be interred in the chapel columbarium in the
small olive orchard that surrounds the tiny church in
the hills. I choose not to take this moment to discuss
the irony of this with Valerie. One of the few things I
know about Leora is that her family were Greeks who
sold produce on the avenues in New York. How she
ended up on the West Coast I don't know, but I do
know she detested any profession tied to agriculture.
Why she would choose an orchard in California as
her final resting place is a mystery to me.

I introduce Valerie to Father Mike, who makes
space for us in his small office adjacent to the sacristy. The sacristy, Father Mike explains, is a small
area behind the altar that holds the clergy and choir
vestments. Father Mike speaks a language foreign to
me, but he is all too pleased to define the terms. I will
attend a service just to see how this all works. Even
Valerie, who—as far as I know—has never been to

church in her life, is captivated. Father Mike senses our utter confusion and asks a simple question.

"How would you like to honor your mother?" He nods at me. "And your grandmother?" He looks at Valerie. "Who would you like in attendance, and what kind of a ceremony do you want?"

Valerie and I look at each other.

"Actually, I've been thinking about this," she says. "We have no family here, but my grandmother had friends, well, she had neighbors . . . we could invite them and . . . " She looks at me. "I've talked to Peter. I know he will want to come and I'd like him to play his guitar."

She turns quickly to Father Mike. "He could play a hymn, or something he's written. Whatever you think is appropriate."

Okay, it's time for me to take back some control here.

I'm starting to picture a Punch and Judy show.

"I think," I say, straightening my spine and sitting forward in the chair, "a private ceremony with just us, and Peter, if you would find his presence comforting, Valerie. We can include Mrs. Dold, who apparently was a good friend to my mother." I direct this last comment to Father Mike.

"No other family?" he asks.

"No sisters, no brothers, no cousins, no . . . no other family."

Valerie shifts in her seat as if she wants to say something. I look at her. "Valerie, we have no other family."

On Wednesday I retrieve Leora's ashes from Spangler's Mortuary. I drive Mrs. Dold up to Saint

Matthew's where we meet Valerie and Peter. It's a bit awkward, but Father Mike disappears behind the sacristy with the box and reappears with an elaborate brass urn. Our little party makes a pilgrimage to the chapel. Father Mike places the urn on a shelf and closes the glass door. A bronze plaque inscribed LEORA DOULIS MORAGA, JUNE 6, 1868–SEPTEMBER 15, 1953 adorns the ledge. Father Mike reads the twenty-third Psalm and Peter strums some unrecognizable tune on his guitar.

Mrs. Dold tells Peter she thinks his music is soothing to the soul. I avoid comment by admiring a spray of flowers set near the side of the columbarium. Bending to touch my nose to a lily, I finger the card and manage to open it. It reads: WITH DEEPEST SYMPATHY FOR YOUR SORROW. ROGER. Not the GE Accounting Department. Just Roger.

We gather for dinner at the Echo—Valerie, Peter, Mrs. Dold, Father Mike, and I. Father Mike tells stories about his last parish. Mrs. Dold extolls the bounty of this year's Italian plum crop and mourns the poor yield she got from her tomato vines because of hornworms. In the midst of a cacophony of conversational bits, my antenna picks up Peter talking about a trip to Spain that Valerie has not mentioned to me. Apparently, she will be leaving soon to oversee the publication of a book she has written. I look at Valerie with a raised eyebrow.

"You've written a book?"

"Oh, it's just my thesis," she says.

Peter opens his mouth to say something, but she continues, a little too quickly and a bit too loudly.

"It's about Spanish literature. That's why it's being published in Spain. No one in the United States

cares anything about the Spanish Civil War's influence on Spanish literature."

"And you do?" I ask. Peter has gone quiet, perhaps sensing that there's more going on here than he
grasps. "I'm sorry," I say to Valerie. "It's your major
field of study. Of course you do."

I have to admit that I have never understood her
fascination with Spanish language and culture. Even
Leora was a little uncomfortable with it. She evaded
Valerie's questions about the Moragas, just as she'd
always been vague with me about my father and
where he came from.

"He died" is all she would tell me. "And he left me
with a young child to take care of and no means to do
it. I made my way in life. I made a good life for you,
Dolores, and here we are and that is that."

I knew my mother well enough to know it was
useless to question her further. So many of the stories she told about growing up in New York and coming out to California had gaping holes. The facts just
didn't add up, so I gave up trying to figure it all out a
long time ago. Not Valerie, though. She wheedled her
grandmother for stories. When Leora got older, the
two of them would sit, heads together, Valerie rapt
over some yarn Leora was spinning. Leora did not
become *mi abuela* or *Lita* until Valerie started Stanford. I don't know what triggered her sudden fascination with all things Spanish.

We all chip in on the bill and Valerie announces that
she and Peter plan to stop by the house for her things
and then return to Stanford. I probably missed an opportunity to try to get to know Peter better. Frankly,
I'm not very interested in a young man whose idea of
offering comfort to the bereaved is to work up a quick

tune on a guitar. I was surprised that he wanted to be a part of our hasty ceremony. What would Leora have thought of a crew-cut baseball player in a Stanford letter sweater serenading her ashes?

As we walk out to the parking lot in the last of the day's warmth, the six o'clock train rumbles nearby. The leaves are turning early this year. Valerie gives me a quick hug and heads for Peter's car, an impressive Packard two-door coupe. Peter lingers, pats my shoulder, and looks into my eyes.

"Thank you for the privilege of playing for Mrs. Moraga's service, Mrs. Carter," he says. He really is an appealing boy. He follows Valerie to the car, stopping to help fold Mrs. Dold into Father Mike's old Willys Jeep. I think she would have preferred to ride with Peter.

I take the long way home through the Los Altos hills. I will return from time to time to the place where we left Leora—

> *The olive orchard*
> *That surrounds a chapel*
> *That contains a columbarium*
> *That displays the brass urn*
> *That now houses my mother.*

An old nursery rhyme picks up the rhythm of my thoughts:

> *This is the farmer sowing his corn*
> *That kept the cock that crowed in the morn*
> *That waked the priest all shaven and shorn*

A voice chants in my head, and in my mind's eye I see two little girls playing on a dusty road.

❧ Dolores ☙

5

SHADOWS

I take the rest of the week off work, Mr. Bradley be damned. I've never been a woman who curses, but I'm surly and short-tempered these days and rather enjoying it. If I'm not careful, I'll lose what few friends I have.

It was Father Mike who pointed out my paucity of friendships when he asked if I had anyone close who could support me during my time of mourning. I did once, but he died.

Henry and I met and married while I was an art student at Chouinard in Los Angeles and he was a signal corpsman stationed at Fort MacArthur. Prohibition and art school mixed a heady cocktail for an eighteen-year- old girl on her own—three parts freedom with a liberal amount of curiosity and a splash of sex. It was the one part conventionality that drove us to the altar and straight into the arms of Uncle Sam. When I married Henry Carter, I wed the United States Army as well.

The Army has a playbook that calls for wives to serve as support troops for their husbands. We quickly discovered that the support position was not a good fit for me, except in the economic sense. I am a lousy folder of socks, but I'm a darn good earner of paychecks. And Henry quietly supported that. We were lovers when proximity afforded and long-distance friends the rest of the time. Shallow work relationships; caring for Valerie, who was born two years after we married; and a repressed yearning for the art career I gave up to marry Henry rendered me the passionless woman I hardly recognize now. It wasn't until Henry died and I found myself alone in my forties that I began to realize I was in the entirely wrong line of work. I have a head for numbers, but not the heart for banking or industry.

Like an old-fashioned circuit preacher, Father Mike drops in on me once a week. He comes by with his Bible on Saturday mornings because I'm the rare woman in my neighborhood who works outside the home during the week. I'm not sure whether his solicitation is solely for my comfort or whether he enjoys our conversations as much as I do. He challenges my take on things in ways no one ever has.

I don't have the benefit of a college education like Valerie does, or the experience of making my way alone in the world like Leora did. The Army became a kind of foster family, providing Valerie and me with the basic necessities—food, shelter, medical care—but it was up to me how much we entered into community life. I detached myself as much as possible from the other Army wives. Like Leora, I've always found most women's chatter frivolous. Unlike Leora, who enjoyed being the center of masculine attention, I never found what men talked about very interesting. The men I met at the bank where I worked before I started at

GE talked about money, business, and baseball. At GE they talk about stocks and bonds and bowling-league scores. Father Mike is really the only man who has ever talked to me about me, and about God, and that has proved to be both a comfort and a concern.

"You didn't notice any changes in Leora?"

I'm not sure what he's after. "Sadly, no, but I probably wasn't looking. What kind of changes are you talking about? I noticed she was getting weaker."

"Ah, yes, but her spirit was getting stronger."

"I don't understand. Leora always had a strong spirit."

"Leora had a strong will. There's a difference."

As the weeks pass, my attitude softens a bit toward my mother. I grew up feeling as if I were a spectator in her life. Her life had all the drama of a silent film, but there was nothing silent about the early Leora. She told me stories about her immigrant parents who sold produce on the avenues of New York. Later they became grocers, but not before Leora somehow made her way west to ply her trade. She had taught herself shorthand, a skill in short supply in the courts out West. Somewhere in the Central Valley of California, she picked up and shed a husband, and then moved on with me in tow to Portland, Oregon, where she took a job reporting trial proceedings. The U.S. District Court put her up in hotels for the months when court was in session in the towns up and down the coast. She loved this gypsy life.

Leora enrolled me in a succession of public schools, but I got most of my education watching my very attractive mother hold a different kind of court. Judges, attorneys, and fellow court reporters loved her. Witty and intelligent, she maintained a high degree of decorum that put them at ease. That ease allowed her to associate freely with the opposite sex without ruining her reputation and losing her job. If there was ever anything untoward about any of her relationships, I never knew about it. She thoroughly enjoyed the company of men—women not as much, me included.

In those days, my mother was the only female employee working in the courtroom. In my job in Palo Alto, I work alongside scientists and engineers who are exclusively male. While I don't have the easy relationships with men that my mother did, it has never crossed my mind to think I might not belong at a desk across the hall from an engineering lab.

I'm recounting this early history to Father Mike when the judgment I have always felt marches out of my mouth. "Leora was not a good mother."

"She was not a bad mother either." Father Mike places a rough-skinned hand on top of mine. I stare at the reddish blond hairs on his muscular forearm. As always, he is wearing a black shirt and clerical collar, but his shirt is short-sleeved in celebration of our mild October climate.

Celebration, it seems, is so much a part of this man's life. It has never been part of mine. Even birthdays were not cause for celebration when I was growing up, except as a matter for reflection by my mother on how close I was getting to becoming employable. But the way Father Mike talks, everything in Christianity is cause for celebration—Christmas and Easter I think I understand, but Advent, Lent and Epiphany? What is that? He talks to me about heart preparation to receive Christ, and celebrations of God becoming a man who walks with us in sorrow and joy. Then he brings my darting eyes to stillness with his steady gaze and makes it personal.

"Dee. You have a litany of grievances against your mother. You tick them off religiously as if you were saying the rosary, but it brings you no peace. Ask your question."

"What do you mean? What question?"

"Just assume there is a God. What is the one question you would like to ask Him?"

"Why did my mother . . . " He stops me right there. "Not a question about your mother, a question about you."

That stops me for a minute. What is it I really want to know? Then it comes to me.

"Who am I? Who are my people? I know there are some Greek grocers somewhere in New York, but who were the Moragas? They are like a poem I memorized when I was a girl. *'I have a little shadow that goes in and out with me.'*"

"Robert Louis Stevenson. I know that poem." He leans back in the kitchen chair.

"I have a shadow family. Sometimes they shoot up tall. I stare at the name painted on the mailbox out in front. Moraga. There's a big tribe out there somewhere, and I'm a missing piece. Other times they disappear. There's just Valerie and I, connected to no one. Why have I been disconnected? That's my big question."

It feels good to say this.

"A noontime child," he muses. "No shadow before; no shadow after."

"If you sketch that child, she lacks dimension."

"Oh, you don't lack dimension." Father Mike stands up and collects the morning paper that I

always let him take with him. "You just need to become aware of your standing in this world, and the
shadows that define you." He seems to be choosing
his words carefully. "Why don't you look for your
connection to the Moragas? I don't think it will be
that hard. Just ask questions and expect answers; and,
pay close attention to what people say and what they
don't say." Then he sets a Bible down on the table.
"You have some reading to catch up on, my girl. In
this book, God will tell you what you need to know.
Start with the Psalms and the Gospel of John."

Father Mike does his two-step down the front
porch stairs. He walks down the driveway and around
the hedge. He's going to check in with Mrs. Dold before he drives off in the old jeep he's parked across
the street. He jokes with me about leaving himself a
clear path to run to his car in case I ever feel like bop-
ping him on the head with a brass bell.

After Father Mike leaves, I stand in the front room
at the table I've set up by the window. I'm turning this
room into an art studio, resurrecting my pencils, easels,
and brushes from the storage boxes in the garage. The
light in this room is perfect. I've pulled out the davenport
that was stashed in the back bedroom, still piled high
with stuff I moved out of our quarters at the Presidio.

My short-lived art career was a trick I played on
Leora. One day I announced that I'd been accepted
at Chouinard Art Institute and off I went. She paid
the bill grudgingly. This was not how she had imagined things, but it did get me out of her hotel suite,
a relief to both of us. It had pleased her that I could
amuse myself with a pencil and sketchpad. It fit our
lifestyle. It was a cheap and portable pastime—but
not a way of life, as she would tell me often.

It certainly was a way of life, one I regretted leaving and deeply missed. What Leora meant was that it was not an acceptable way of life to a single mother looking to unburden herself of a teenage daughter who was outgrowing the confines of their migratory nest.

But this is exactly what Father Mike told me not to do. I need to put down the litany of my mother's sins and pick up my sketching pencil while the light is still good. Artfully arranged in front of me is the altar of objects I've removed from Leora's nightstand: the brass bell and the framed photo of Leora and Valerie. I spill the Anglican beads around them. Then I move toward the table to adjust the frame. The photograph is askew, revealing something behind it. I take the frame apart and discover what looks like a postcard.

The evening fog is moving in. I close the front door, turn on the floor lamp by the davenport, and sink into the softness of its pillows, pondering the front of the postcard. It is a picture of a grassy valley with mountains in the background. Sheep graze in the distant foothills. The largest animal wears a brass bell. Sky dominates the setting. It would be a lovely but boring picture were it not for the dominant image in the right foreground. A large workhorse stands over a smaller horse reclining on the grass, feet folded under its young body, head facing the distant mountains. The standing horse seems attentive to its young charge—and protective. There is a breathtaking intimacy in this scene.

I turn the postcard over. There are words scribbled in pencil on the back. They are hard to make out, but finally I do.

Ardi galdua atzeman daiteke, aldi galdua berriz ez.

And a translation.

The lost sheep may be recovered, the lost time cannot.

And a signature.

We are fine. Al

The postmark indicates the card comes from somewhere in Spain. The message must be from my father. The Moragas must have come from Spain.

I'm puzzling over my discovery when the phone rings. I'm not paying much attention when I pick up the receiver.

"Hello, Mrs. Moraga?" The voice is female, with a slight accent.

"No, this is Mrs. Carter. Mrs. Moraga is . . . was . . . my mother."

"Has something happened to Mrs. Moraga?" The voice sounds genuinely anxious.

"Who is this?"

"I'm so sorry, Mrs. Carter. My name is Pilar Ibarra. I'm calling from the Basque Relief Agency in Bakersfield. Mrs. Moraga has been a very generous donor to us over many years, but it's been some time since we've heard from her."

"Miss Ibarra, my mother passed away last month."

"Oh no, I am so sorry for your loss, Mrs. Carter. May I offer condolences on behalf of our agency? We truly did appreciate the years of support your mother gave us."

This is awkward, but I have to ask. "Miss Ibarra, to be honest, I was not aware that my mother was at all interested in your agency. May I ask what kind of work you do?"

"Of course." Pilar launches into a lengthy description of the history of the Basques, their troubles during the civil war, and their migrations to Idaho, Nevada, and California's Central Valley. Something about this has an oddly familiar ring. It sounds like the subject of Valerie's thesis. Could Valerie have known about these people?

"Thank you, Miss Ibarra." To extricate myself from the conversation I add, "If you would like to send me a brochure on your agency, I will consider making a donation in memory of my mother."

"Thank you so much! And, Mrs. Carter, we would love it if you would visit us in Bakersfield. We have a large Basque community here. We have a festival every year that attracts people from all over California."

I mumble something and ring off. Then it occurs to me that I didn't ask the question I should have. Why was my mother interested in the Basques—so much so that she donated regularly for years to their cause? But I know the answer.

Sunday morning I stand on Mrs. Dold's front porch after she returns from church. When she catches sight of me, she moves slowly to the front door.

"Come in, Dolores," she says in the slow, breaking way that elderly women speak. I adjust my quickstep tempo to her slow waltz shuffle as I follow her into the kitchen, watching the little blue and yellow and pink flowers on the old cotton house dress she's changed into swish across her broad backside. Cinnamon, cloves, and apples are boiling in a pot on the stove. The mouthwatering aroma blends with the sharp smell of a recently lit gas stove. She's making batches of apple strudel.

"You'll wait until my strudel is out of the oven." She has just taken over my day. "I'll fix tea while we're waiting and we'll have a nice visit."

Why don't I come over more often? She's alone all day in this house, but she doesn't seem lonely. She keeps busy with crocheting, writing letters to her sisters in Germany, placing orders from her seed catalogs, and amusing the neighborhood cats—a parade of regulars who like the German songs she sings as she pours cream into the collection of chipped pottery bowls she lays out for them.

She tells me about Mewsie's new kittens, Truman's abscess, and the soaking poor Felix endured when the nasty next-door neighbor turned a hose on him.

"Cats pee in gardens, what are you going to do?" she says. Then she extols the improvement in her own Gertie's sleek coat due to a daily dose of cod liver oil. I wait for her to take a breath and then I jump in.

"Did my mother ever talk to you about my father?" I study her face for a reaction, but there is none.

"Your mother was not one to dwell on the past." She gets up and goes to check the strudel baking in the oven.

"Actually, she talked a lot about the past. In her last years, she told me stories about her travels with the court after I went to Los Angeles, but she never said anything about her years in the Central Valley."

"Oh, I don't think she spent a lot of time there. Your mother didn't like farm country. She much preferred the coast."

"My father was a farmer?"

"I don't know what he was. She never talked about him to me. We talked more about her days in New York, because I came through Ellis Island too."

"My mother came through Ellis Island? I thought she was born in the United States."

"Well, she was very young when she came over from Greece. She had no memory of the old country. She always said her life began when she first saw the Pacific Ocean."

"Do you think my father was with her then?"

"No."

I'm beginning to badger her. It was this way every time I questioned my mother. No matter how I broached the subject of my father, her mood would sour instantly and I would pay for it in invented lists of chores or long afternoons of silence. Best to let it go, but I can't this time.

"Was his name Al?"

"His name was Alonso. That's all I know, really."

She cuts us both a slice of strudel and comes back to the table with two plates of flaky pastry nestled under a thick glistening sauce that enfolds the tender apple slices. "Many of us have left a past behind that we don't want to talk about. This is such a wonderful country. You should look ahead, Dolores. You are young. You don't have your mother to take care of anymore. Valerie has her own life. Find a good man and get married again."

My mother didn't do that. She was very young when she was left alone with me. She could have married again.

"Was my mother really married to my father?"

"Of course she was married to your father."

"How do you know?"

"I know, Dolores. This won't get you anywhere. Let your mother rest in peace and go live your own life." She pats my hand and then goes into the other room to retrieve her latest piece of crochet to show me.

I start back across the street toward home, but end up walking around the block to settle myself down. I take long steps, swinging my arms, filling my lungs with air scented by honeysuckle vines. Why do I care so much? Ask the big question, Father Mike said. Okay, God, here it is. Why did the connection break? What else did I lose when I lost my father? It's not what Leora lost or threw away that concerns me. It's what I lost that I want to know.

❧ Dolores ❧

6

LETTING GO

*M*y old Chevy is making a noise I don't recall having heard before. I pull into my parking space at work, lift the hood, and look at the engine. I don't know what I'm looking for, but soon my co-workers arrive and form a consultative circle. Could be a bad spark plug, says one. Or a loose fan belt, says another, who joins me under the hood. Roger walks up and mingles with the head shakers.

"Dee, when was the last time you changed your oil?"

It's just like a man to assume I don't maintain my car. I've been the sole maintainer of all motors, gadgets, and parts for years. I did not expect all this attention when I put my head under the hood, but I might just as well have raised my skirt and showed some leg, for all the commotion. Mr. Bradley walks by and frowns, and our little party disbands and heads into the building.

My performance review is today and I'm preparing myself to be upset. Mr. Bradley does not like me, that is clear. When I show up in his office, his secretary gives me a fleeting wisp of a smile and nods her head toward his closed door. He is ready for me. Elaine returns to the task of putting a new roll of paper in an adding machine as I enter the sanctum and sit down in a chair with an unusually deep seat. I am a fairly tall woman, but I've sunk so low into my chair that my knees have popped up. Like an awkward Alice in Wonderland my feet barely touch the recently vacuumed carpet. Mr. Bradley occupies a leather executive throne that creaks and rolls each time he shifts position. It's distracting.

"Dee." He opens a manila file folder and runs a finger down a page only he can see. "You've been with us, what? Three years."

"That's right, sir."

"And . . . " It is obvious he has not reviewed my record. He closes the file and levels his gaze at me. "I'm just going to tell you what I think, Dee. I think you are in the wrong line of work."

My heart starts to thud as I picture myself in a Depression-era bread line. But as always, I use what I know to take command of the situation as best I can. I take an invisible deep breath, lift my chin, and sit still for a full minute. This makes Mr. Bradley fidget.

"I can only assume, Mr. Bradley, that you have something in mind."

The man has ignored the list of my accomplishments that Roger and I worked up. I'm in no mood to listen to his personal grievances, so I execute an end run.

"And frankly, Mr. Bradley, I'm glad to hear it. I think I've made many contributions to Accounts Payable—you have the list—and I would welcome a new assignment." This is risky. I give him my perkiest smile.

"Ah, a new assignment isn't exactly what I have in mind, Dee."

I have underestimated this man. "I'm putting you on probation."

My self-confidence plummets, but I rally. "You've never indicated you are unhappy with my work, Mr. Bradley." I pull myself to the edge of the chair so I can straighten my spine, not an easy feat because the scooped seat has molded me into a hunchback.

"It's not your work, Dee, it's your commitment. I have big expectations of you. You are exactly the kind of woman we would like to see move into a supervisory role one day, but you seem to have other priorities. You have to be prepared to make sacrifices if you want to grow with us."

"Sacrifices." I nod my head thoughtfully. "Beyond staying late, working through lunch, taking work home . . . " He stops me by holding up his hand.

"You miss the point, Dee. A woman with less experience could do your job. You haven't made any effort to learn new skills to make yourself more useful to us. We aren't about just doing the same job over and over, we're about improvement. Now this is what I'm looking for in the next six months. Take some courses in accounting and contracts. Something just may open up for you. In the meantime, I want you to start training Sally on the invoicing."

"You're giving my job to Sally?"

"I didn't say that. But we need someone who knows how to do your job when you take time off, like you do every time you have a death in your family."

"Well, that's not much of a worry, Mr. Bradley. I haven't got much family left."

"Well, I'm sorry if I offended you, Dee, but there's no need to be impertinent. I think we're done now."

I get up to leave and he adds, "Oh, I forgot, you will be getting your cost-of-living raise, so don't worry about that. Take my advice and in six months your record will be clean."

I force myself to say "Thank you, Mr. Bradley." I walk past Elaine with flies of anger buzzing loudly around my head. Am I about to have a stroke?

Roger finds me in the employee lounge.

"You look pale. It didn't go well?" He pours himself a cup of coffee and sits down beside me. I give him all the details.

"Dee, that's not all bad, you know."

"He's going to give my job to Sally," I hiss at him through gritted teeth. "How is that not bad?"

He cocks his head and looks at me. He raises an eyebrow slowly, expecting me to answer my own question. "We both know you are overqualified for the position you have. You are doing the work of a bookkeeper. You are better than that."

His words thrill me and scare the hell out of me at the same time.

"Let's take a break and go for a walk, Dee."

We walk down the tree-lined boulevard on Page Mill Road next to pastures where well-groomed horses graze, the sun glinting off their muscled bodies. Hoover Tower looms in the distance. It's deceptive, this quiet Valley of the Heart's Delight. The barons of industry who created this landscape imagined themselves to be gentlemen farmers, I suppose. It looks like they achieved a perfect balance of agriculture, education, and industry, but the agriculture is vanishing fast.

We walk in silence and then I begin to talk. I'm talking mostly to myself, and Roger is listening.

"The truth is . . . " I look hard at the truth. "The truth is that I like the safety of my job, but I don't like my work. I have never liked this work. I don't know how I got on this path or why I've stayed so long." What has possessed me to reveal so much of myself to my supervisor? Roger makes no comment; he just listens as I barrel on.

"I don't hate the work. It satisfies my need for routine. I seem to have a high tolerance for boredom. That sounds just awful."

This is more than I have ever said to Roger about myself and my feelings. I've revealed very little about myself to my coworkers. At this moment, though, I want to reach out to this man so I keep going.

"Do you know, I once had a job offer from Walt Disney? He invited me to be part of a team of illustrators he was putting together in a new art studio. My job would have been to sketch backgrounds, landscapes for the action. It sounded so exciting and fun."

"Why didn't you take it?"

"I married Henry, and his career became my career. I was an Army officer's wife, keeping things going while he was away, raising our daughter, supplementing our income with whatever jobs I could pick up that were acceptable to the Army brass. Being a bank teller was acceptable."

"But you hated it?"

"No, I didn't hate it. I didn't mind the work, especially when I worked in the city. The financial district was a beehive even during the war, everyone coming and going, working together to keep things in good repair and growing."

"All to the feed the queen," he mused. "Who was the queen, Dee?"

I am silent for a minute. "I suppose it was the American Dream—peace, prosperity, and happiness."

"Were you happy?"

"Except for the fear that Henry might not come back from the war, I think I was. I never doubted we would win, that we would recover and rebuild. I felt a part of that."

"And now?"

"I don't feel part of anything meaningful. When Henry deployed to Korea, I moved out of the city to take care of my mother. Henry died overseas. Valerie became a permanent fixture at Stanford. Somewhere in there, I lost my life."

We walk back to the GE building through the parking lot, pausing for a moment by my car. Roger folds his arms across his chest and looks at me.

"Let me ask you something. Do you still sketch?"

"Funny you should ask. I haven't for a long time, but I've recently started to again."

"We should go back in now." Roger thumps his hand on the trunk of my car. "We haven't finished this conversation though. What say we go to dinner one night this week?"

I'm torn between embarrassment at having talked so much about myself and curiosity about where the conversation might lead. "I'd like that," I say, in my best approximation of a professional tone of voice.

We head back to our desks. My anger, frustration, and fear over my review have subsided to a low-level fever that will require treatment but not hospitalization. My energy is returning.

My car won't start when I leave work in the evening. Roger hears me calling a tow truck from my desk and offers me a ride home.

"I live in the opposite direction you do." I've heard he has a house in Redwood City. "I can catch a ride with Sally." I look over at her empty desk. "We have things to talk about anyway."

"She left at noon for a dentist appointment and then she took the rest of the day off. I think you are stuck with me."

We supervise the towing operation and then I walk with him to his late-model Buick. "Mmmmm, still has the new car smell." I'm trying to keep things light.

"I was in a meeting late today with Ralph Cordiner," Roger announces.

"You mean Mr. Cordiner, the president of GE?"

"Yes, we were discussing a remodel of the building that involves placing artwork in the lobby and halls. He wants to get local people involved, so I volunteered you."

"You did? That sounds like an interesting project. Thank you, Roger."

"His secretary will call you and get you plugged in with a committee of employees who are working with the Palo Alto Art Commission."

I've never done anything like this in my life. Part of the reason I went to work was to avoid participating in the community life of the Army posts. I never did fit into the extensive social fabric that formed the military weave. Most of the wives were from the southern part of the United States or from the Midwest. They regarded anyone from California with suspicion. My art school background cast me as bohemian in their minds, exotic and dangerous. I liked that.

I learned from watching my mother that you can play a part that makes it easier to get along in social situations. She played the part of a knowing observer of life, a raconteur who could always be counted on to help a group of legal professionals pass a pleasurable evening.

When I worked for the bank, no one cared a hoot about what I did in my off hours. On weekends, I sketched at the harbor while Valerie played in the park across from the marina. I put away my pencils after Henry died, but I think I lost my way long before that.

"I've lost you," Roger says, as he navigates past the hedge and pulls the Buick into my driveway.

"I'm sorry, it's been a long day." I open the car door and then think to turn to him with the obligatory invitation to come in.

"I would, but not tonight. You pick a place for dinner on Saturday and I'll pick you up at five." And then he leaves.

I wander down my driveway in a trance and stand there for a minute. Cars go by and pull into driveways, children are playing in front yards, and the clink of dinner dishes being set on tables wafts through open windows. I open the mailbox and reach inside for a stack of mail. How will I get to work tomorrow? Tomorrow would not be a good day to tell Mr. Bradley that I will be unable to make it in, tempting though that is.

The neighborhood settles down around me and the crickets start up. In the house, I open a back window and the frogs in the creek join the evening symphony. I sit down at the kitchen table with the mail. Sorting the mail is a daily ritual. I search for the most beguiling piece to open first, and I find one: a Hallmark card addressed in a bold hand using a heavy ink pen. It's not writing I recognize. The postmark is Bakersfield.

I tease the envelope open and pull out a condolence card. Under the embossed text of sympathy, words written in a shaky script float in front of my eyes.

> *Dear Dolores,*
> *I am sorry to hear that your mother has passed. She was a remarkable and courageous lady. I hope you are well.*
> *Iban Moraga*

Is this my father? But the signature is not Alonso Moraga, it's Iban Moraga. It's an old man's handwriting, so perhaps he's a brother or cousin? He must be. I now seem to have relatives living only a few hours away. Surely it won't be that hard to track Iban Moraga down. He must have heard about Leora's death from Pilar at the Basque Relief Agency.

I'm exhausted. I turn out the lights and head for bed, where I spend a sleepless night imagining a tearful family reunion. An aging uncle introduces me to my father—a ranch hand struck by lightning while repairing fences, blinded and unable to write to me. No. A rich and noble uncle takes me to my father's grave; he weeps as he tells me about his brother who died young, leaving a brave, pregnant widow who vowed to make her way in the world without help from the relatives who disapproved of the marriage.

It's almost dawn when I finally fall asleep.

❧ Valerie ❧

7

BIRD IN THE HAND

I'm ready to go. Yesterday I finished my packing and picked up my airline tickets from the travel agency for my trip to Barcelona. I leave today. Mother and I managed to make it through Christmas—she by working a lot and me by reading a lot. On Christmas Eve, she dragged me to Saint Matthew's and on Christmas Day we saw *Roman Holiday*. After the holiday Mom and I had, I'm ready for a holiday of my own.

Thanksgiving and Christmas are always awkward because none of the women in our family cooks. Now that we are a family of two, it's easier. My grandmother always wanted to go out to eat, but Mom and I didn't have the heart for it this year. I'm not sentimental about holiday traditions, but where am I headed when I spend Christmas with my mother in a movie theater filling up on popcorn and Coke instead of Christmas dinner? Perish that thought. I'm headed to Barcelona!

Mother will be by in a few minutes to take me to lunch at Clarke's and then to the airport. Peter was in a pout because he's not driving me, but we said our good- byes last night. I don't want to get on the airplane with a tear-stained face. If I think too much about how good it felt to be in his arms, to snuggle up to his chest and smell his skin, pungent and full of promise—a giggle begins in my throat, then spits like rain out of my eyes. Damn, Mom is outside.

"Where did you get that big dent in your car?" If we talk about her, she might not notice I've been crying. Her old Chevy has a new dimple in it, like she's banged her car into something. Turns out I'm right. She ran up a curb and hit a post-office box in San Bruno. She seems accident-prone these days. We chat a bit and then I ask her what she was doing in San Bruno.

"Well, I want to tell you about that." We're pulling into the parking lot of the purveyor of the world's yummiest hamburgers. "But let's get a table first."

The burgers on the broiler smell so fresh they must have been cows an hour ago. At Clarke's you smell the beef, not the grease. The meat juices baste your chin; it's like eating heaven on a bun. I am going to miss this.

I munch my way through my burger as if I were a ground squirrel digging to China while my mother goes on and on about the hours she is spending at the National Archives in San Bruno. I start to listen.

"So this library is where people go to research their families, and there are lots of records from the Central Valley. I've figured out that Iban is likely Alonso's brother and that something happened that caused Alonso to disappear, but I've got Iban's phone number now and I'm going to call him this weekend."

I don't know what she's talking about. My mouth is full so I raise a finger to get her to slow down, but she barrels on.

"I found an item in a Bakersfield newspaper on microfiche about an incident that involved some sheepherders and some cattle ranchers. Iban and Alonso are mentioned, but the photograph is fuzzy and I can't make it out, so I'm going to call Iban and ask him. Or maybe I will get in the car and drive to Bakersfield where he lives. But I will probably call first."

"Whoa, whoa." I put my hamburger down on the plate and wipe my chin with my napkin. "Who are these people?"

"My father and my uncle," she smiles triumphantly. "Our family. I'm sorry, I've gotten way ahead of myself." And then she tells me about the mysterious phone call and the condolence card.

This is not good. I had no idea she cared at all about the family history. I'm the one who cared. I never got anywhere with her when I asked questions, so when Leora got older and lost some of her defensiveness—not that my mother noticed—I spent a billion hours pulling bits and pieces of information out of her failing mind. That information I wove into the story that is about to be published in Spain, the country of my grandfather's origin. It's the reason I majored in Spanish literature and became fluent in Spanish—so I could think and write like a native. Leora's story captivated me. My grandfather came from the Basque region, which has a fascinating history. But my grandmother was never as forthcoming as I would have liked. And now my mother seems to know more about it than I do. And less.

My mother pushes an envelope across the table toward me. "This came in the mail last week. I have an uncle Iban who is still alive. My father's name was Alonso. I'm guessing he's dead, but I'm going to find out."

I'm not that worried that my mother will find out what happened to Alonso. I'd like to know that myself. What I'm worried about is that she will find out the big news that Leora dropped on me a few months before she died. My mother had a sister. From what I pieced together, that sister may actually have been my mother's twin. What did Leora expect me to do with that information?

All I know is her name was Alaya. I based the sisters in my book on my mother and her phantom sister. If my mother ever gets a hold of my book, there are enough personal details in it that she'll know I didn't make the whole thing up. She'll know that I knew something and that I kept that information to myself.

"Don't you want to finish your hamburger?" My mother has finished her burger and filched all my pickles.

I fake a look at the big clock on the wall. "No, we really need to get going. I don't want to miss my plane."

"You're right." She stands up and reaches for her purse. "Let's go."

On the drive to the airport, I brace myself for questions. I'm expecting my mother to ask me how long I plan to be gone, what I've done with my student apartment, what my plans are for when I return—the whole drill—but she doesn't. Instead, she starts in about this Roger guy that she's having dinner with tonight.

"Roger, the guy who called you from work after Lita died? Roger, the guy who sent flowers to the memorial service? Who is he, anyway?"

"He's my supervisor at work. He's been a big help to me in trying to figure things out."

"What kinds of things are you trying to figure out?" The juices from my burger are mingling with the juices in my stomach and it's not a happy stew. "Should you be so cozy with your boss?"

"Well, you know my review at work was not what I expected, and I'm re-evaluating what I really want to do with the rest of my life. Roger is very good at asking questions that open up possibilities in my mind. But Father Mike is the one who really got me started examining the path I've been on."

Suddenly I'm sorry I have an airplane ticket in my purse. And glad.

Mom runs a red light. Fortunately, her lapse in driving judgment goes unwitnessed. She's chagrined though, and that gives me an opportunity to gain some control.

"Mom, I've asked Peter to check in on you while I'm gone, so be nice to him, okay?"

"Why on earth would you think I need to be checked on?" She is offended. "I'm not a pet poodle you've left home while you traipse through Europe." She's gathering steam. "Valerie," she says sternly, "I have my own life. I don't need to be 'checked on.'"

"I know. I'm sorry." And I am. It is more comforting to me to think about my mother's routine days, going to work, working in her garden, living like a nun in the Los Altos bungalow she's inherited, safe and predictable, than to think of her making weekend trips on Highway 99 to Bakersfield and returning, breathless with adventure, to the arms of some guy named Roger.

"So tell me about Roger." Father Mike is not the man to worry about.

"There's nothing to tell. He's a friend."

"Don't you have any women friends?"

She thinks about that for a minute. "How funny you should ask. Father Mike asked me the same question. No, not really. But I'm working on that."

We are at the airport.

"Honey, if it's okay, I'm going to let you off at departures. I'm not confident I can find my way out of here if I have to park."

But you are confident enough to meet a stranger named Iban. "That's fine, Mom."

I swing my duffle bag out of the trunk and hug her good-bye. "Thanks for the ride, Mom. I love you. Take care."

Hours later, I settle into my seat and open my copy of *Sexual Behavior in the Human Female* by Dr. Kinsey. Seated next to a grandmotherly type with a knitting project on her lap, perhaps the title alone will deter unwanted conversation.

The book turns out not to be as engaging as I thought. As the plane rises into the sky, I close my eyes and think about what's ahead. Professor Stegner has encouraged me to continue to write fiction, so I've been playing around with Lita's story. In my Spanish saga of two young sisters raised in vastly different cultures, my grandmother makes a brief appearance— she's what E. M. Forster calls a flat character. In the new piece I'm working on, I'm letting her have her own voice. These are her stories after all.

Lita tried her hand at writing about the court cases she recorded. You would think they'd be boring, but they were anything but. Love triangles, murders, Indians, thieves, gallants, and fallen women. My grandmother was like the Charles Dickens of the Wild West, weaving morality tales in which brave women succumb to folly.

She gave me a pile of her typewritten stories before I left for Stanford. They took a good deal of rewriting, but now I've got a collection of short stories I've written in Spanish packed away in my duffle bag that I plan to put under the nose of my publisher. I've edited Lita's memories and come up with some great yarns. Spanish readers love a good western, especially one set in California.

Those stories are gold. It was easy to extract what probably happened to Lita early in her life that gave her the strength to raise a child alone and the moxie to succeed in a man's world.

I am a lot like my grandmother. She was an independent woman, very adventurous and passionate about life. She wouldn't give up what she wanted for a man, like my mother did. Mother would like me to get married. She wouldn't like to see me marry Peter though. She doesn't seem to like him, but she doesn't really know him.

The knitter in the aisle seat keeps bobbing her head and then jerking awake. I have to go the bathroom, but I don't want to disturb her. So I concentrate on Peter and the foolish thing I did before I left. I let him give me an engagement ring. I was caught by surprise when a smallish diamond ring nestled in a velvet box arrived with the cheesecake at Rickey's Studio Club. How could a girl refuse such a gesture?

To the applause of the other diners in the restaurant, I let him slip it on my finger. I took it off this morning, wrapped it in tissue, and stuffed it into my wallet with my coins.

I turn a page in my book. As much as I cherish Peter, I would like to feel free to meet a romantic Spanish man, maybe fall in love and live in Spain for the rest of my life. If she had made a different choice, I'll bet my grandmother would have been happy living in Spain. It is, after all, where we come from. Well, Lita came from Greece, but her *apuesto pastor* was a Basque.

If I don't meet an *apuesto* Spaniard and I do come back to Stanford, I want Peter to be waiting at the terminal. I probably do love him, but he's such a boy. Who knows what he will do with his life. If I become a famous author though, we could marry and he could do what he likes.

❧ Dolores ❧

8

CATCH AND RELEASE

Driving home, the void Valerie leaves in my life whenever she leaves the country begins to unnerve me. I don't see her that much, but knowing she's close by is a comfort. Father Mike said to think about making room in my life for people. We are created for community, he told me. Why I haven't done this?

Trawling the past is like the catch-and-release fishing that Henry tried to interest me in—unsatisfying for me, at best, and very annoying to the fish. As the traffic whizzes by, I do it anyway—fish for memories. I pull one up, examine it briefly, then let it slither back downriver to school with my other fishy memories, a little scarred for the experience but intact. I see a friendless little girl dropped off at a circus-themed birthday party. She's wearing a short trapeze-artist costume and enjoying the breeze on her knees. She watches the balloon twister who is dressed like a clown. She doesn't know she's friendless—well, she does now that she's been caught and released.

Before this, she was just happy to be invited to the party. Now that she's been examined and found wanting, her eyes have been opened. There are big fish and little fish in this river. She's one of the littlest and she swims alone.

All this thinking about fish reminds me that I need to stop at the nursery and get some fish emulsion to amend the soil for my spring garden. I may be a little fish in lonely waters, but this year I'm going to cultivate a big garden. And I'm going to cultivate some new relationships. Starting with Iban Moraga.

I've been putting off the call all week. As I unlock my front door, the invisible hand of Father Mike pushes firmly on my back, urging me forward. I repeat his advice like a mantra in my head: *To change your path, you have to sacrifice something in order to get something better.*

This week I gave something up. I gave up all pretense that I will ever take a finance class or a management class. Now I'm determined to get something. I'm going to get the truth out of Uncle Iban.

An old man with a slight Spanish accent answers. "Iban Moraga?"

"Yes."

"This is Dee Carter, um, Dolores Moraga. Leora's daughter?"

Silence.

"Dolores. How are you? You got my card. I imagine you got this phone number from the same person who gave me your mother's address."

"Pilar."

"Yes, Pilar. She is like the Bell Telephone operator for the Basques. She makes it her business to keep track of everyone."

"How long have you been in touch with my mother, Uncle Iban?"

"Well, it hasn't been easy. She moved around a lot in the early years. Every so often, she'd send me a photograph. You've grown up to be a beautiful woman, Dolores. And you have a lovely daughter."

"You know a whole lot more about me than I know about you." I was trying to keep the conversation free of emotion, but my hands are starting to shake. I plant my elbow on the table to steady the telephone receiver and glue my knees together.

"Yes, well, I made a promise to your mother that I would never try to see either one of you. She needed to make a new life for the two of you. I understood that."

I wait for him to go on.

"But she's gone now." He sounded sorrowful and hopeful at the same time.

"So, would you be willing to see me?"

"I would welcome the opportunity."

This is more than I had hoped for. I don't want to say anything to cause him to change his mind, so I offer to come to him. He seems genuinely pleased and suggests Memorial Day weekend. That seems a bit far out to me, but he says something about doctor appointments and a Basque festival.

After the call, it's time to dress for my weekly dinner date with Roger. I'm shimmying into a black slip, fastening my stockings underneath and rehearsing the feel of his fingers against the back of my neck as he helps me into my coat. This is the first time I've admitted to myself that dating is what Roger and I are doing. Of course, I don't know what he thinks we're doing. Maybe he's just being uncommonly nice to a coworker who's standing on the precipice of unemployment. But I'd bet good money he feels the same tug in his gut that I do when he lays his arm across my lap reaching for a map in the glove compartment without apologizing.

Office gossip has it that he isn't married. He lives in the town where he grew up, Redwood City, in the house he grew up in. That raised my suspicions until he mentioned that his mother and father were buried in Union Cemetery and that he'd moved into the family home to fix it up for sale. He's been at GE since he graduated from Cal Berkeley, except for time served in the South Pacific on an aircraft carrier. He's forty-four, two years younger than I am, a shameless fan of the San Francisco Seals baseball team, and a private pilot—he flies a little Ercoupe that he's been trying to get me up in for weeks now. He's never mentioned any women in his life except a sister on the East Coast, who is the mother of a niece and nephew he's very fond of. If he were a pedigreed puppy, I would adopt him and take him home. But grown men are a little harder to accommodate into your life.

At dinner I tell Roger about my plans to drive to Bakersfield in May.

"Dee," he says, with barely contained excitement, "let me fly you there!"

I start to sputter.

"No, listen." He pulls out a ballpoint pen and begins to draw a map on his napkin. "We can fly east over the Coyote Hills through the Sunol Pass, over the Altamont Hills and down the Central Valley. It's a two-hour flight."

I open my mouth to protest.

"An old college roommate of mine owns a ranch in Bakersfield. He has plenty of room to put us up." I raise an eyebrow, but he keeps going. "And he can lend us a car."

"How do you think this would play back at the office if it got out?" As it is, we've been careful not to discuss our dinner dates within earshot of anyone in the department. He deflates like a cheap balloon. My vocal chords tighten. I raise my hand to my throat and run my fingers over the soft skin under my chin. This man has just offered me champagne and I've ignored the crystal flute and headed for the water cooler.

Go after something you want. I want this man. I shake my head, reach for my wine glass, and raise it slowly and deliberately to my lips. Then I shoot Roger a sexy look over my cabernet. "Let's do it."

We discuss the trip all through dinner. Back in the car, Roger reaches for something in the backseat and drops it in my lap.

"I have a present for you."

"Roger," I protest, tearing into the brown-paper wrapping. "Roger!"

"It's the Canon IIB." And then he launches into a discussion of viewfinders and interchangeable lenses.

I'm speechless. The words *I can't accept this gift* enter my mind, but only for the briefest of moments. This is something I never would have bought for myself, although after finding the cash bundled in the back of Leora's closet, I certainly could have. I'm still trying to work out why my mother maintained the charade that she had no money when she had thousands of dollars shoved in purses and stacked in shoe boxes.

I measure the weight of the camera as I turn it over in my hands. "If I can master this, it will take me new places in my artwork."

"You can bring it along on our trip and we'll play with it." Roger gives me a wink and a crooked smile as he places his hand over mine and gives it a squeeze. What else does he want to play with on our trip? I thought our relationship was going to grow slowly. He's only ever given me a respectful kiss goodnight. *It's a camera,* I tell myself, *not lacy black lingerie.*

Tonight Roger doesn't wait for a kiss at my front door. He pulls me over next to him in the car and kisses me slowly and deeply, lips parted, his mouth traveling down my neck, his fingers playing across my collarbone and straying just to the top of my breasts. I'm wearing a push-up bra that has positioned my breasts to receive this attention with enthusiasm. His breathing deepens. I look up into those deep-set brown eyes. His black curly hair is loosening from the bit of Brylcreem he uses to keep it in place. Nothing is in its usual place tonight. If I don't put a stop to this right now, Mr. Roger Russell is going to get it all— right here and right now—for the price of a camera. To my surprise, he stops first.

"Let's not do this in a car in your driveway," he murmurs softly into my ear. I'm slightly offended that he assumes that I was about to throw myself into the backseat of his car like a teenager. We both sit up and adjust our clothing.

"This feels like being back in high school," I say, "not that I did a lot of this sort of thing in high school."

"Me either, but that's a conversation for another time. It's late and I need to get going and let you get some sleep." He gets out of the car and comes around to open the door for me while I gather up my purse and my new camera. I thank him for dinner and the gift, give him a quick kiss goodnight, and send him on his way.

I had not imagined I would ever have to puzzle out the politics of sex again. I was what they call these days a "technical virgin" when I married Henry. We'd done everything but. We were faithful to each other. During the Depression and the war, the long separations and the short times we lived together, our energy was consumed with getting through the bad stretches.

After Henry died, I figured that this part of my life was over. But it's the fifties and things are different. There is such hope in this country now. People have done without so much for so long that they are eager to rebuild their lives and enjoy all the new gadgets science is developing for our modern society. Tonight has shown me that this part of my life is not over. Still, I'm a woman living alone, thinking more about God, and I need to be cautious about what I do.

Sunday morning I go to church. Before this, I never saw the point of going regularly. The few times Leora made any reference to God, she spoke of "the man upstairs." That gave me the feeling that God is someone who will have to be reckoned with at the appropriate time. He's keeping the books on my life and someday he will reconcile my account.

When I was a teenager, I sometimes went to Catholic Mass with my girlfriend Betty. She religiously took confession every Saturday morning and topped it off by attending Sunday morning Mass to atone for what she did on Saturday nights with her boyfriend.

We ate lunch at her house afterward, and she would share the thrilling details of what she and her boy-friend had done. There is nothing I read in *True Confessions* that I didn't hear from Betty first.

I'm not sure what to expect at St. Matthew's. I want to sit in the back of the church and let the liturgy find its way through my scattered thoughts. Iban Moraga, Pilar Ibarra, and Roger Russell tumble over one another in my head. Father Mike proceeds down the aisle waving a censer this way and that. The sweet smell of incense fills the air and calms me. The words *blessed, peace, grace, mercy* and *love* echo in my heart, and Iban, Pilar, Roger, and even Leora take a comfortable seat somewhere in the back region of my brain. We sing hymns that call to mind the Psalms I have been reading.

Even confessing my sins brings me peace. I am beginning to discover that I have a lot of sins to confess, and it has nothing to do with what Roger and I did in his car last night. It has everything to do with the lifetime of grievances I have nurtured against Leora for her subterfuge and her lies. Even her protestations of poverty—Henry and I bought her a house when we couldn't think of buying one for ourselves because we thought she had no money. I laughed and laughed when I found that small fortune in her closet. Then I sorted and counted the bills, and deposited them in the bank.

I have spent so much time trying to imagine what she was hiding all those years about my father's family. But I think I'm ready to let it go. *Let something go and get something you want.* Uncle Iban will have a story to tell me. I will let what he tells me fill in the missing pieces of my life and I will be satisfied. I don't want to spend any more time poring over old census documents and newspaper records in the genealogy library trying to figure it all out.

I will use Leora's life savings to get the things I want. It turns out that I am like Leora in more ways than I thought. I will find a new career. I will seek out adventures. Unlike Leora, I'll seek adventure in love.

The service is over. I can't tell Father Mike I enjoyed his sermon. I didn't even hear it. I do shake his hand at the door and tell him I enjoyed the experience. He gives me a hearty pat on the back and moves me in the direction of the coffee and cookies. Today I found a sanctuary, a place to reflect. I leave, more in command of my spirit than when I came. I will come again.

I'm in the process of moving out of the front room everything that doesn't support my artistic endeavors. First to go was the telephone table and its central distraction, the telephone. I gave the table to a thrift store and plopped the telephone down on my kitchen table. The only furniture besides the piano I've left in this room is the davenport. I love to stretch out on its roomy cushions and lean back into the pillows I've piled at each end. When the days warm up, I can loop one leg over the low back and set my other leg on the floor to let the breeze from the open door cool my thighs.

I wheeled the TV into what used to be Leora's bedroom. It is now my sitting room, my reading room, and my TV room. I've never lived in a place that I could decorate solely to my own taste. What a jolt to discover that, like my mother, I have made no accommodations for guests.

The piano broods in the corner. It hasn't been played in years, not since Valerie practiced on it when she visited her grandmother. I have nowhere to move it though, and no desire to make a decision about its next life. It does make a handy place to display my sketches and collages.

I am engaged in sorting through photos to place in a collage when a sharp rap on the screen door startles me. I look up and see a woman about my age wearing smart red capris and a candy striped crop top. She calls to me through the screen.

"I am so sorry to bother you. I'm collecting in the neighborhood for the American Heart Association." She laughs. "I'm the one who couldn't figure out how to say no when they called. A dollar would be fine." I invite her in and go to get my purse.

"I should introduce myself," she says as she takes my dollar and hands me an envelope to fill out. "I'm Laura McMillan. We just moved into the old Ghirardelli place on the corner."

All the houses in this neighborhood below the golf course were built as weekend cottages for people in the city to get away from the fog and enjoy a summer picnic by the creek. That particular house was the vacation home for the ten Ghirardelli children. They even had a pony. Now that the commuter train stops at the corner crossing, people are moving down from San Francisco and staying all year. Farm animals aren't as numerous, although the occasional rooster still runs in the road.

"I know what you're thinking." Laura laughs. "We must have a passel of kids to want a house that big, but we don't." She offers no further explanation. "Say, is this an art studio?"

Mrs. McMillan is what my mother would have called a bit forward, but there is something refreshing about her. I follow her as she walks around the living room admiring everything she sees.

"Oh, just look at this." She stands in front of a series of collages I have arranged on top of the piano. "They are beautiful." I detect just the slightest southern accent in her speech. North Carolina, I'm betting.

"And what a sweet piano!"

This gives me an opportunity to hold up my end of the conversation. "Do you play?"

"I used to, but I don't get much chance to anymore. I had to leave mine in Raleigh when Fred took a job at IBM."

"Well, this piano never gets played and it is probably badly in need of tuning, but if you ever want to come down and play it, I'd enjoy hearing the music."

"Really?" She looks as if I have just offered her the moon. "Oh, that is so nice of you. I would just love that. I brought all my music with me. I have some George Gershwin tunes I was working on. Do you like him?"

"You can play Gershwin? You are welcome anytime." We make arrangements for her to practice at my house on Tuesdays and Thursdays, right after I get home from work.

"Do you happen to play bridge?" she asks. "

As a matter of fact, I do, but it's been awhile."

"I have a bridge group that meets on Wednesday afternoons at my house. We're adding a second table and we need a fourth. Oh, but you work, don't you." She gives her short blond bob an imperceptible shake.

"Not for much longer, I don't think." I promise to let her know when I'm available and she gives me a hug.

"I'm so glad to have met you. We seem to have so much in common." And then she's out the door to finish her canvass of the neighborhood.

Have I been a little too quick to let the likes of Laura McMillan into my life? But a woman friend outside of work might be just what I need. My probation is up tomorrow. I am due in Mr. Bradley's office at eight AM.

✺ Dolores ✺

9

STOPS AND STARTS

I'm standing outside Mr. Bradley's door waiting to be summoned. Elaine looks up and gives me a broad smile.

"So what's this I hear about you and our very attractive Mr. Russell?"

Elaine poses as harmless, but she has a nasty bite. She curls in her corner, watching the web she has spun. She sucks the juices out of her unsuspecting victims, snaring tasty bits of gossip that she turns into poison and shares with the chosen members of her A list. Mr. Bradley is at the top of that list.

"I don't know Elaine, what are you hearing?"

She laughs. "Oh, I'm hearing about intimate dinners for two, expensive gifts . . . "

"I can't imagine how you are hearing that. Is Mr. Bradley about ready for me?" I turn my back on her and move to the window. I focus on trying to pick my car out in the parking lot several stories below. My face is burning.

"You know, dear, you might want to take a little advice from someone who has your best interests at heart." She rises from behind her desk and an assassin's breath prickles the hairs on the back of my neck. "Office romance is against company policy." She is standing behind me now.

Mr. Bradley's door opens. "I'm ready for you now, Dee."

I walk through the door. Whatever Elaine thinks she knows, she has shared it with her boss.

I look at that devil of a chair waiting to swallow me up and move instead to the small conference table in the corner. I drag a smaller chair over to his desk and perch on it. He looks annoyed but says nothing. He makes a show of looking at my file.

"I understand that you have trained Sally and that she has taken well to the duties of accounts payable. Good. Good." He snaps my file shut and levels a look at me from his hooded eyes. "However, I don't see anything in your personnel file that indicates you have taken any of the classes I suggested."

"That's because I haven't." "And why haven't you?"

I say the words I've been preparing to say for months now. "Mr. Bradley, I've thought about what you said, and you are right. I'm in the wrong line of work."

This catches him off guard. It isn't what he expected or what he's used to hearing from intimidated employees. He rises to his feet and paces by his window.

"Well, Dee, you understand that we are not trying to push you out of the company. Not at all." He gives me a horsey smile, showing his perfect white teeth and a little gum. "We want to groom you for a bigger position."

I hate that image. It's as if someone were slapping me with a stiff brush and braiding my tail. I rise from my chair as well. It's time to negotiate.

"Mr. Bradley, I can give you as much notice as you would like, but I'd like a good letter of reference from you. I performed the job I was hired to do well, and I think I deserve that. I can write it myself, if you wish, and give it to you for your signature."

His smile disappears. "That may be, Mrs. Carter, but there is the matter of violating company policy."

Here it comes.

"On the other hand, if you choose to fire me, I can collect unemployment and that will work for me also."

Mr. Bradley shakes his head slowly and walks around the desk to stand beside me. He places a hand on my shoulder, looks down at me, and gives me that gummy smile again.

"Well, Dee, if you are determined to leave us, I can only wish you well in your next venture. I'll have Elaine prepare a letter of recommendation for you and let's say two weeks' notice, shall we?"

"That will be fine." A mix of terror and relief shudders through me like an earthquake; terror at what destruction may have just occurred and relief that it is over and done.

As I am leaving, he adds, "Mr. Russell and I will miss seeing you in the office, Dee. It may not be your line of work, but you are good with figures." He looks me up and down. I let that go.

On my way out the door, I flash a brilliant smile at spider woman. Then I return to my desk and start organizing files and boxing up my personal items while trying to be inconspicuous. Roger is in the hallway conferring with Sally. It has been awkward, seeing him in the office every day after what transpired in his car a few weeks ago. In another month, we will fly to Bakersfield. By then I expect I will feel freer to enjoy his company. Hopefully he will feel the same way. Oddly enough, it never occurred to me to tell Roger I was planning to quit. Now he will hear about it before I have a chance to talk to him.

Laura, music in hand and ready to practice, is on my doorstep when I arrive home.

"You must be tired after working all day." She follows me into the house and heads for the piano. "Just ignore me and do whatever you do to unwind after your day." She sits down on the piano bench, uncovers the keys, and begins to run scales.

I change into a pair of knit pants and a loose sweater, and go to the kitchen to pour a glass of wine. I pour one for Laura and place it on top of the piano. She smiles and nods, but continues with her warm-up. I sit down on the floor with a box of photos and begin sorting. I'm creating templates for collages that will help me tell my family story. I'm looking for a poetic visual effect rather than the prosaic documentation that scrapbooks contain.

Any family history has holes in it. Like the words in a poem, a photograph can have many meanings. Perhaps encouraging the heart to see the questions instead of feeding the mind with the answers can produce a texture that is more truthful. Collage is the perfect medium for this kind of storytelling. It's stories I'm after, not history.

I'm absorbed in my task when Laura squats down beside me, the glass of Chablis in hand.

"This looks like you," she says, placing a freshly manicured finger—Hot Baby Pink, I'm guessing—on a blurry black-and-white photo with a crinkle-cut white border. It's a photo I've been puzzling over. It appears to be me standing next to a man I don't recognize. I look to be about eighteen years old in the photo. The clothes are odd. The girl is wearing a nondescript dress that I can't identify as anything I ever wore. The man has his arm around her shoulder. Surely this is a photograph I would remember posing for, because that is most definitely my face. Or maybe it's my mother. Maybe we did look alike. People say we did, but I never could see it. Maybe the man is her father. It doesn't look like it was taken in New York, though. Maybe they were on vacation. Too many maybes; I turn the photo over and look for something stamped on the back to identify it. Nothing.

"If that's not you, it's your twin," Laura says.

My mouth drops open and I look at the photo again. "I don't mean literally." She laughs. "They say everyone has a twin. Haven't you ever had anyone say to you 'I know someone who looks exactly like you'?"

"Yeeesss."

"Do you have any sisters who look a lot like you?"

"Not that I know about."

I'm not going to solve this one tonight. I put the photo in a pile I plan to take with me to ask Uncle Iban about. There aren't many. Leora was not a picture taker. She didn't hang on to many photographs either. There are a couple of baby pictures of me but no birthday photos, school pictures, or graduation portraits. I appear in only a few photos with my mother and different groups of strangers—attorneys posing at dinner tables for photos taken by hotel photographers; well-dressed women posing in front of art museums or civic monuments.

"I should go. Fred will be wanting his dinner." Laura stands and hands me her empty wine glass. "Thank you for this." She stretches out her arm and sweeps the room in a dramatic gesture that takes in the art, the wine and the piano. "Your salon inspires me."

On her way out, she mentions the bridge game again. As much as I like the game, whiling away the afternoons playing cards seems far too decadent to this working girl, even though I won't be working much longer. I decline.

What will life be like when I no longer report to a job? Will I be allowed to continue consulting on art acquisitions for GE's lobby when I'm no longer an employee, or is that a bridge I have burned?

Despite the years I've spent dreaming of having time to pursue my art, the looming reality is frightening. I know how to do a job. I have no idea how to pursue a career in art. Leora pretty much convinced me it wasn't possible. I wasn't at Chouinard long enough to figure it out either. Too many years have passed since the offer of employment at Disney. The world of animation is now beyond my sketching ability.

Roger is being slow to react to my defection. I hide out in my office, organizing my work and writing notes for Sally, who will be taking over my job when she returns from vacation. My two weeks' notice is almost up by the time he finally strides into my office, shuts the door behind him, and sits down in a conference chair. I look up. He crosses one leg over the other, folds his arms across his chest, and leans back in his chair looking at me as if I were a recalcitrant child whose antics mystify him. Then he places both feet on the floor and leans forward, jabbing his index finger on my desk as if he were squashing a bug.

"Why did you quit without telling me, Dee?"

"You encouraged me to start thinking about my options. Why are you so surprised?"

"Because I'm your supervisor and you should have come to me first."

He's got me there. That's the protocol—why didn't I follow it? Because Elaine is right, office romance is a bad idea. This factored into my decision and I chose romance over the office. Once I cast Roger Russell in a romantic role, I ceased to think of him as my boss. I can't get out of this office fast enough.

"Roger . . . Mr. Russell . . . you are right. I should have discussed my plans with you."

He stops poking my desk and curls a fist under his chin, regarding me with a frown. The sleeves of his white dress shirt are rolled to his elbows and I'm staring at the tanned skin of his forearms and the soft layer of black fur that sleeks across the hard muscle of his arms, muscle that wasn't built pushing a pencil against a ledger at GE.

Finally he says, "Dee, it's just that I expected you to confide in me."

"Roger, I have confided in you. I hope I can continue to confide in you. Would you have told me to do anything different?"

He is silent for a time. Then he shakes his head. "I will miss seeing you every day."

I raise an eyebrow.

"But we'll make up for it on the weekends." He stands and slaps the palm of his hand on my desk.

"Be packed and ready to go. I'll pick you up Saturday morning." Friday evening, when I should be packing for my trip to Bakersfield, I am sitting in Father Mike's little office after vespers.

"You told me to let something go. I let my job go. You said I could change my path. I leaped off the path and now I don't know where I'm going. You said I should go after something I want. Well, maybe what I want doesn't want me! It's possible I'm not artist or girlfriend material. I'm staring into an abyss here, Father Mike." I pull a tissue out of my pocket and blow my nose.

He leans back in his chair and interlocks his fingers into the shape of a church. Thumbs crossed tightly against the doorway to his little chapel, he places the spire of his two pointer fingers against his lips.

"I didn't tell you to do it all at once," he says. Then he laughs. "Dee, this is what faith is, being sure of what you hope for, even though you don't see it. What is your biggest hope?"

"Oh, God." I slump in my chair. "That's a start."

"Let me start with my small hopes, okay? I hope I haven't made a mistake quitting my job. I hope I can make art make sense in my life. I hope I can continue to see Roger and see where our relationship might go without having things get all messed up."

"You are hoping to fall deeply in love?" "It's not just Roger."

"I know that. Let me ask you a couple of questions. Do you have artistic talent?" "Yes, but—"

"Then it will make sense. Artistic ability is a gift from God. He will use it. Maybe not in a way you imagine, but in a way you will recognize and rejoice in. Roger isn't a married man, is he?"

"No! Of course not, at least not now. Maybe in the past? I don't know."

"Good. Find out as much as you can about him . . . from him."

Out the high window of Father Mike's little cell the sun is going down, glinting through the olive trees. The last of the faithful few have departed. Father Mike leans across his desk and gives me his famous, soul-piercing, *listen up, soldier* look that puts me on alert.

"Here's the most important thing, Dee. I want you to try this spiritual exercise." His words compel me to sit up straighter in my chair. He reaches for the Bible that occupies a prominent spot on his desk and flips through the pages until he finds what he's looking for.

"I want you to assume there is a God. Ask Him to bless you. Ask Jesus to guide you. Ask the Holy Spirit to empower you. Then watch what happens."

"Where do you come up with this stuff, Father?"

He slides the Bible across the desk and swivels it around in front of me, placing a meaty finger underneath a chapter title. With his other hand, he taps two fingers to his heart.

"Read the book of Romans," he says, "and listen."

My eyes follow to where his finger points. I nod my head and change the subject.

"Roger is flying me to Bakersfield this weekend to meet my Uncle Iban, my father's brother."

"Good." He rises from his chair and packs some papers into his briefcase.

"We are staying with a friend of Roger's, on a ranch." He looks at me, eyebrows raised.

"All on the up and up, Father. Roger made a point to tell me that I will have the guest cottage all to myself."

℀ Dolores ℀

10

HALF TRUTH

Roger and I lift off from San Carlos Airport in his Ercoupe.

"This baby cruises at 114 miles an hour." He is in his element, explaining aeronautical details with the passion of a small boy. "No rudder pedals—it's like driving a car in the sky."

But it's a small car; he's allowed me only one tiny suitcase. My discomfort in the cramped quarters dissolves when I look out of the canopy above us and see puffy clouds waltz by. The bounty of the Central Valley is below us, welts and wales of rich dirt offering up cantaloupe and corn, strawberries and squash. It reminds me that my own garden lies fallow and neglected. I make a mental note to do a late-season planting as soon as I get back.

I look over at Roger. He's relaxed and happy.

"Don't you just love this?" he says, patting my knee.

I doze a little until we begin our descent. Rising thermals catch us and now it's more like a tango than a waltz. Roger has explained that we won't be landing at Meadows Field. Instead, we are looking for a private airstrip on his friend's horse ranch near Gorman. He's flying low, spreading maps out on my lap, and scanning for landmarks.

"Do you see a wind sock down there anywhere?"

I try to imagine what such a thing might look like. In the distance I spot a stretch of road and an orange tube on a pole. There are industrial buildings at the end of the road. I point in their direction.

"Is that what you're looking for?"

Roger leans over to look. "Good girl. That's it." He sets up for a landing, navigates a strong cross-wind, and brings the little plane down. Frankly, I will be glad to put my feet on the ground.

A Land Rover with the keys under the mat is waiting for us. We climb in and Roger turns to me. "Okay, Dee, I figure it's about a half hour drive to where your uncle lives. You can drop me by the house and go on by yourself, or I can drive you to your uncle's house. What do you want to do?"

As tempted as I am to let Roger do the driving, I want to see Iban alone. Roger is happy to spend the afternoon with his college pal, so I drop him off at the door of a spacious ranch house and head for the highway. Just past the time I should have eaten lunch, I pull into a long driveway at the edge of Los Padres National Forest. It leads around to an inconspicuous house nestled in the trees. When I step up to the door, sudden fatigue feels like sandbags weighing down my shoulders. Am I doing the right thing?

Before I can muster strength to knock, Uncle Iban opens the door. We stand there a moment, taking each other in. He is a spare man in a dress shirt and neatly pressed pants. Decades of sun damage map his face. Brown eyes sparkle from within deep folds of skin; he welcomes me with a loose-lipped smile. He stands very straight for an old man.

"Dolores, what a welcome sight you are. You look just like your mother." He grabs both my hands in his and shakes them. "Come in, come in."

The house is as neat as the man. He indicates that I should sit at the dining-room table, which is set for a meal. There are three place settings. The steamy sweet aroma of roasted peppers mixes with pungent basil, thyme and rosemary, and the weight on my shoulders lifts.

"My dear, I had Pilar cook us up some *menestra*. We Basques do wonderful things with vegetables."

As if on cue, Pilar scoots out of the kitchen holding a hot bowl of stewed artichokes, peas, green beans, asparagus, Swiss chard, and ham. She sets it down before it can burn her hands. Pilar looks to be about Valerie's age. She is wearing slim black pants and a black boatneck sweater with an Italian silk scarf wound around her neck. Her thick black hair is caught in a ponytail. Beautifully arched black eyebrows accent a sloe-eyed gaze that is friendly if a bit guarded. Iban also has these arched black eyebrows even though his hair has gone completely white. Perhaps it's characteristic of Basque people.

"Dolores, I asked Pilar to be here because I want you two to get to know each other." He teases me with an elfish smile.

I can't imagine why he would want that, but it's obvious he is fond of her. My stomach is grumbling. Iban chatters on while we all stand behind the chairs at the table, shifting our feet.

"Pilar is the glue in our community." He reaches over and pats her shoulder. "She knows all our stories."

"Then she knows more than I do." I try to keep the petulance out of my voice.

Pilar breaks the tension by pulling out her chair. Iban and I follow her lead and seat ourselves. "Let's eat and then you two can talk while I clean up the dishes."

It puts me more at ease that she won't be hanging around while I try to pry information from my uncle.

The stew is wonderful and I'm completely drawn in by Pilar's description of the Basque Festival in Bakersfield that she wants to take me to this evening. Everything about their culture is foreign to me.

"Where exactly is Basque?" I direct my question to my uncle.

"The Basque land spills across the Pyrenees Mountains and extends to the Bay of Biscay." Iban chases a green bean down his chin and catches it with a hunk of bread. He sits up tall and puts his elbows on the table. "We Basques have our own language and customs that date back centuries."

Pilar picks up the conversation. "Many of our people came here to Bakersfield during the Gold Rush. But they come today because a repressive government denies us freedom."

"The Moragas have been in California for a long time." Iban raises his voice and jumps right into the family history. "José Joaquín Maria Moraga went on expeditions with Juan Bautista de Anza. Did you know that he founded the Presidio in San Francisco? But I know that's not why you are here today. You want to know about my brother, your father."

Pilar begins clearing the table and disappears back into the kitchen.

"Let's go sit in the living room, and I will tell you our story." Iban settles into a leather chair and I take a seat on an ottoman facing him. He begins.

"Alonso and I came to this country as young men. We missed the Gold Rush, but we found opportunities in the sheep business. People think all Basques are sheepherders, but that's not true. We do know sheep, but it's not as big a business in Navarre because our country is so small. In America, the herds number into the thousands. The bosses couldn't hire enough of us to tend sheep camps and herd the sheep in this valley. We did it for the money, so we could go back to Navarre and buy an apartment and set up a little business."

This part of the story is familiar. I studied California history, but I don't want to break Iban's train of thought. While I'm wondering when he will get to the point — what happened to my father — he jumps the track with his story.

"Our countrymen made a good living supplying lamb for food, first to the miners and then to the people who came here for the oil. Basques are enterprising. With the money we worked so hard for, some of us bought land, became citizens, became ranchers or oilmen, and grew rich."

I look around Iban's house. It's obvious he was one of those people, but what about my father? Iban notices that I'm frowning and picks up his story.

"It was not our intention to become shepherds, but it was the work that was available to us when we arrived. It was hard, lonely work that didn't pay well, so you have to do it for years before you save up enough money. Dolores, let me tell you what it was like.

"A man walks a herd of one thousand sheep up into the high country where they graze for months. When he's in the high country, he has no contact with other shepherds. His job is to take care of his sheep and keep them safe from predators. Maybe he has a horse, but often not. He has a dog. He sleeps in a small trailer and has to figure out how to feed himself. The food was so boring, beans and no meat. I was lucky though, the boss liked me. Sometimes when he came to my camp to bring supplies, he would bring me a fresh chicken. Then I could practice my English.

"The life suited me for a time. I read books and made plans about what I would do when I came down from the hills. I got two weeks of vacation every year that I used to take English classes so I could get a better job.

"For my little brother Alonso, this life was not so good. I guess he thought that the opportunities would come faster. He didn't expect it would take years, saving pennies, denying pleasure. We saw each other once a year when we brought our sheep down and the boss took them to market. We always met up at the Basque picnic in Bakersfield. That's where your father met your mother."

I sit up on the edge of the ottoman to encourage him to keep going with this part of the story.

"Leora had taken a train out from the East Coast to look for work. She'd spent some time in Los Angeles with an aunt, but her dream was to go to San Francisco. She was on the train heading north when it derailed in Bakersfield. The railroad company offered to put the passengers on a bus or put them up in a motel to wait for the next train. The train ran through Bakersfield once a week in those days.

"Leora thought she'd rather stay in a motel and wait for the train instead of being bounced through the desert on a bus. Our Basque picnic was a big event in town. She wandered over to see what it was all about. Alonso spotted her right away. A summer with the sheep had taught him that wolves are always watching; he wasted no time in offering the young lady his protection. That didn't go over very well at first. You know, your mother left New York to escape the protection of a large family."

That does fit with what little I know about my mother's history and character. I shift position on my perch, tucking one leg underneath the other. Pilar walks into the living room balancing a pitcher of water and some glasses on a tray. Setting the tray on a low table by Iban, she pours two glasses and hands me one. Then she sits down in a chair at the far end of the living room. Iban continues his story.

"Yes, Leora had many older brothers who had their ideas about how an unmarried sister should conduct herself. Leora didn't like any of their ideas. That's why she arranged a visit to her aunt, knowing that it would be only a detour around her brothers on the way to her real destination. It wasn't overbearing brothers or a derailed train that stopped her in her tracks though; it was Alonso.

"He was a handsome man, my brother. He talked her into looking for work in Bakersfield even though she didn't want to stay. She needed an ocean, she told him, and he promised her they would go to the coast as soon as he made enough money. They were married in the Noriega Hotel."

Iban pauses to drain his water glass. He seems a little out of breath. His forehead is shiny with moisture. His health is not as good as I first thought. He continues his story though.

"Well, Alonso didn't want to go back to herding sheep. He had a wife to support and a baby on the way. Leora wasn't happy finding herself pregnant so soon, and Bakersfield was not the kind of town where a young woman could find anything other than menial work anyway. I was tired of walking the sheep up the trail too, so I started on a plan to get us out of the sheep business. I wanted to help my brother move his family to new pastures, where they might have a better chance to be happy.

"This stretch of country was sitting on oil fields the likes of which you could not imagine. Knowing exactly where it was and getting the land rights to drill was the problem. The boss, he was smart. He helped the oil companies buy up land cheaply and then short-leased it back to folks. His family, they are all property managers for the big ranches now. In those days, all the land was under lease agreements. When a family had to sell a house, the oil company had first right of refusal. They owned the land. They'd buy the house for cheap and tear it down. Houses got to be in short supply. People didn't really understand what was happening, but they knew that housing prices were depressed even though the shortage should have driven things the other way. Alonso and I got ourselves into the demolition business, tearing those houses down and letting the land just sit."

Iban stops here and wipes his eyes. Pilar goes into the kitchen to get more water for him. He drains another glass and hands it back to her. She puts a hand on his shoulder and he reaches up and pats it, almost as if he were drawing courage for what he is about to tell me.

"Dolores, Basques are hardworking people who do what's right, generally speaking. In this country, doing what's right doesn't always get you ahead. You have to do what's smart. We thought the smart thing to do was to figure out how to get the oil out of the ground. I'm not so sure we were wrong about that. Oil made this valley rich."

Iban seems to be heading off in a direction I'm not interested in. I want to know what happened to my father. I shoot a glance at Pilar, who has retaken her chair in the corner. She sits patient and still, waiting for Iban to go on, and he does.

"One afternoon we were tearing down a ranch house and some outbuildings that had been built on open grazing land. Rumor had it that a group of cattlemen had been forced off the land because the oil company wanted to do some drilling in the area. An angry group of drunken cowboys rode out and found the two of us pulling down a bunkhouse. The boss and his boys came riding up about the time the cowpokes started shooting. The boss raised his rifle and *boom, boom, boom.*" Iban makes a shooting motion with two long fingers. "Those three cowboys were dead."

"The boss didn't want to bother defending himself in court over this, so he worked up a scheme where Alonso would take the blame. It was pretty farfetched. Everyone knew that the Basques didn't generally carry guns. But he offered my brother money for his family, money for passage back to Navarre where Al wanted to go anyway. He said that the whole thing would blow over and Al could come back. He promised me an office job with better pay, enough so I could send some money to Al."

"Why me?" Iban says, when I raise an eyebrow. "Because I spoke good English."

Iban tells me that Alonso had asked the boss if he could take his wife and daughter and the boss said he'd arrange for their passage. My father boarded a bus for New York believing Leora would follow. I'm not surprised when Iban tells me Leora opted for a train ticket to San Francisco instead.

"When she left, she told me she didn't think she would ever see Alonso again," Iban says. "She planned to start a new life and told me not to contact her. Alonso made plans to return and look for her, but before he was able to make the trip, the United States closed the borders to Basques. They didn't reopen them until a couple of years ago. By then, Alonso had died."

"What did he die of?"

"He caught valley fever his first year in California. It didn't bother him much at the time, but twenty years later he had a relapse. He developed an abscess in his lung that killed him."

Iban begins to rub his shoulder. Pilar stands, comes across the room, and kneels down beside him. Gently she says, "Your Uncle Iban caught the fever too. His case is milder, but it bothers him from time to time."

She takes one of Iban's hands into her own and massages his palm. "Iban, I'd like to take Dolores out to the picnic now. She can come back tomorrow and you can talk some more then."

I dig my hand into the pocket of my jacket and feel for the photos I have brought with me. Then I look at the clock. It's five PM.

"I should call my friend," I say. Pilar points me to the phone, and she and Iban talk quietly while I call the number Roger gave me.

"Dee, I'm glad you called." Roger sounds relieved. "It's getting late and I was getting worried about you."

I explain what the plan is and ask if I can keep the car for the evening.

"How about if we come out and meet you at the picnic? It sounds like fun."

I don't really want to meet any more new people or have to explain anything to Roger tonight, but I can't think of a good excuse to turn him down when he's gone so far out of his way for me.

Walking out to the cars with Pilar, I say, "My uncle seems to have done well for himself."

"Yes, he worked for the oil industry for forty years. They gave him a good retirement."

"Why do you know so much about him?"

"It's my job, Dolores. The Basque population is small, but we keep close tabs on one another. I studied at UC Berkeley under an anthropology professor who is following the diaspora of the Basques in the Western United States. We have an ancient history that's worth preserving. What you'll see tonight, the singing, the dancing, the costumes, the language . . . that will speak to you in better ways than I can."

❧ Dolores ❧

11

WHOLE TRUTH

We drive to the fairgrounds in separate cars. In the parking lot, I see Roger getting out of a truck with a stocky man wearing jeans, a tooled leather belt with a massive silver buckle, a plaid shirt, and a cowboy hat. He gives Pilar a hearty wave. It does seem that she knows everyone for miles around. Roger introduces me to Xabier Mendoza.

"Where is Maria tonight?" Pilar asks.

"Babysitting the grandkids. They're all sick." Xabier and Pilar lead the way. Roger strolls beside me, hands in his pockets.

"How did things go with your uncle?"

"I found out that my father herded sheep, fleeced people out of their homes, and fled the country because he got involved in a shooting. He died in Navarre before the war. How was your day?"

Roger is silent for a few minutes. Then he says, "Xabier told me a little about your father's story. It didn't sound like he knew what he'd gotten into."

"What? Everyone knows this story except me?"

"Not the whole story. Xabier is an attorney who works on land-use cases. I used to wonder why you could drive forever through this area and see so few houses. I figured maybe it was all ranch land, but Xabi says no, it's the land grab by the oil companies. People can buy and sell houses, but not the land the houses sit on. Value is in the land, not the house, so . . . "

I wave my hand in the air and walk on ahead of Roger. My head aches and I don't want to talk about this anymore. Roger trots to catch up with me.

"Dee, what your father got caught up in was the animosity between the sheepherders and the cattle runners. He was pretty much an innocent bystander."

I shake Roger off and disappear into a crowd of people filling their plates with caramelized ribs that you have to wrestle off the bone with your teeth.

There is so much wrong with this story, I don't even know where to begin. It seems I can't get a straight answer about my father without getting a whole history of the Basques. It doesn't make sense to me that two people who had decided to build a life together would go off in two different directions and be content to never see each other again. That's not something I would have done. Then it hits me. That's *exactly* what I did.

When the country wasn't at war and Henry was posted all over the United States, how many times did I decide not to go with him? Other Army wives pulled their kids out of school, packed up their lives, and followed their husbands. Not me. I'd lived like a gypsy as a child and I was determined that Valerie would not live like one. Her home was in San Francisco. I could argue that I sacrificed my marriage for my child, but that wasn't true either. Like Leora, I let my marriage go because I didn't like the life.

The barbeque is about finished and I move with the crowd toward an outdoor stage. Men in white shirts, black vests, and white pants with red bells laced around their calves stand in formation with women in red skirts, white blouses, and black aprons. The men wear red or black berets, the women white bandannas. Accompanied by the somber tones of a mandolin played by a young boy, the dancers move in intricate patterns as a flag bearer enters their midst. The flag has ribbons of white and green on a red background. The ceremony ends when the dancers fold themselves on the ground like supplicants and the flag bearer waves the flag gracefully over their bodies. Then musicians break out tambourines, accordions, horns, pipes, flutes, and drums, and the dancing begins in earnest. It's very balletic; dancers jump and kick, twist and twirl. There are line dances, circle dances, and stick dances; some dancers hold arbors, some hold implements I can't identify. They dance with joy but not abandon. Their steps are schooled. This is tradition being passed down.

I have lived my whole life in sophisticated cities and towns on the Pacific coast, always aware of other cultures. The melting pot we call it, each ethnic group lending flavor to the stew we call America and losing some of itself in the process, but that is progress. What I see here does not fit that picture. This is an ancient culture that will not melt. They do not dance for their entertainment or mine, they dance for the preservation of a people. Few will ever set foot in Basque lands again, but they carry its landscape in their hearts. Pilar was right. This speaks to me. Somewhere I have people who are connected with this thrilling display of national pride. The stress of the day falls away, replaced by a yearning and a peace beating to the rhythm of a hunger and a satisfaction.

In the distance, Pilar leaves Xabier and Roger chatting in a circle of men. She pushes her way through the crowd to find me.

"I want to introduce you to some people." I follow her to where the older women are sitting on folding chairs. "This is Dolores, Alonso Moraga's daughter."

She places her hand at the small of my back and applies a comforting pressure. I've never heard myself spoken of as some man's daughter. The women smile at me and chatter in a strange language that sounds like nothing I've ever heard. I try to identify it. Spanish—no, Welsh—no, Hungarian—no.

"They are speaking Euskara, the Basque language," Pilar explains. One of the women speaks to me in English.

"I remember your pretty mother," she says, "and you girls."

"You must be thinking of someone else," I say. "I'm an only child."

"Oh no, dear, I remember. You are Leora's daughter, am I right? She had twins—identical twin girls."

❧ *Valerie* ❧

12

ALIVE AND WELL

I'm in love. I'm in love with Spain and with Gibert Borrell, the son of my editor, Esteve. Señor Borrell invited me to his home for dinner one evening and Gibert was there. I must be clairvoyant because Gibert is the tall, dark, and handsome man I dreamed about. He is finishing medical school at the University of Barcelona and he loves literature and poetry, so much so that he is trying to decide whether to enter medical practice or give it up and become a novelist. Of course, his father is trying to discourage him from giving up medicine for writing, but Gibert is very talented, the kind of man who could succeed at whatever career path he chooses.

I don't get to see him much because he is on call at the hospital most of the time. I've told him that I want to explore the Basque region. He's been very obliging on his days off, although there are areas he has warned me to stay out of because a few Basque nationalists are stirring up hatred against Spain. Franco has decreed one language and one flag for the whole country. The Basques are fierce in their desire for autonomy.

It is such a beautiful region of Spain, tucked against the Pyrenees like a cherished child snuggled up under the arm of a protective mother. At least one weekend a month I climb on the back of Gibert's motor scooter and we speed along the winding roads that connect farms and fields, orchards and vineyards, old forests and sheep trails. The rest of the time, I'm making the revisions to my manuscript that Esteve requires. I'm almost done and that's a good thing. My money will run out at the end of this year, and I'm going to have to return to Stanford.

Esteve has asked me to come to his office today to meet the illustrator who is doing the cover for my book. She has expressed particular interest in my work, he tells me, and has asked to meet me. What a process this has been. Publication is scheduled in four months. Esteve wants me to stay another year to help promote the book. I want to, but I don't see how I can.

The publishing house office where Señor Borrell works is in a medieval building in La Ribera. I wait until three PM, when I know they will be open again. Esteve spots me coming through the door and waves me into his office. Behind him, a woman with her back to me is spreading out some drawings on a counter under the window. Esteve leaves the room and the woman turns to look at me. She looks at me for a long time before she extends her hand across the desk and introduces herself.

"I'm Alaya Moraga. I'm very happy to meet you, Valerie."

I stare at her in amazement. She has my mother's face. Alaya is, in fact, almost an exact replica of my mother. She's about ten pounds lighter and her dark hair falls in soft curls almost to her shoulders; other than that, they could be twins. And now I know where my story came from, not from my head but from Lita's heart.

"My grandmother only hinted that she'd had another daughter. I wanted it to be true. I wrote the story as if you were still alive, but I made it up. I had no idea you ever really existed or if you did, that you might still be alive."

I am talking way too fast. I'm holding my breath too, because the edges of my vision are starting to go black. I place a hand on the desk in front of me to steady myself, and draw in a breath. Alaya stands very still and regards me with a small smile, as if I'm some exotic bird she has long hoped to view. She seems very satisfied. I, on the other hand, am increasingly annoyed.

"You've read my book." She nods. "My mother hasn't read it. She knows nothing about you."

Alaya moves around to the side of the desk and sits on the edge. "Do you know why my father left the United States with me?"

"No, Lita didn't tell me, only that he left her alone to raise my mother."

"That's not the way it happened." Alaya comes to her feet again. She picks up a pencil and taps the eraser end sharply on the top of the desk. "The details aren't important, but my father was involved in an incident where men were killed. He didn't shoot them, they were attacking him. His boss shot them. To protect himself, the boss made my father take the blame for the killings and then sent him back to Spain to avoid prosecution." Alaya sits back down on the desk, adjusting the wide belt that circles her slim waist as she continues her tale.

"There was no time for him to talk Leora into leaving with him, hardly time to even explain what had happened. Dolores and I had just had our first birthdays; we were still babies. Leora panicked. She told him she could not possibly provide for two of us by herself. He told her that Iban would help her care for us if she stayed in Bakersfield until she could make arrangements to travel to Spain, but she wouldn't agree to stay. They decided to split us up. Alonso would take me back to Spain, where he had family to help, and Leora said she would take Dolores to her aunt in Los Angeles. Only she didn't. She went to San Francisco and got a job where she traveled. It was years before Iban discovered where she'd taken my sister."

"How could she do that?" The grandmother I loved so much could not be so selfish and cruel.

"They were very young, Valerie. They didn't know each other very well. My father told me that Leora felt she'd made a mistake in tying herself to a man who'd only ever walked sheep on a trail and had no real prospects. He had promised her he would work a different job and save money and they would leave the desert."

I walk around the desk, pull out Esteve's big leather chair and fall into it. "What has your life been like?"

"My life has been good. My father was always grateful that your grandmother let him take me back with him. He loved me very much. My grandparents helped him raise me. I stayed with them during the months that he walked the sheep. Before he died, he made good on his promise to Leora, that I would not be a shepherd's daughter."

"How's that?"

"He purchased his own herd of Latxa sheep and a small farmhouse. We made Roncal cheese and sold it to the neighbors. After the war, my cousins sold the cheese to small grocery stores and restaurants, even to some restaurants in San Sebastián and Barcelona." She laughed. "We became quite famous for our cheese."

"But you're an artist."

"Yes, there was enough money for me to go to art school. I did sketches for our cheese labels long before we were in production. My father encouraged me to use my talent."

"My mother went to art school too."

"I know. And speaking of that, I will admit that I came here today to meet my niece, but we do have work to do."

"But there is so much more I want to know! How do you know so much about us, and we know nothing about you?"

"Patience, Valerie. Let's choose the art for your book cover. We will have plenty of time to talk later."

We move to the wide window ledge and turn our attention to her sketches. She has represented my theme well. I choose a drawing of two horses separated from their herd. Alaya has sketched the horses in bas-relief to the landscape behind them and placed them in the lower right corner of the scene. The older horse appears to be attentive to a changing season. A wind catches his mane. He stands guard over a smaller horse reclining in the grass.

"Tell me about these horses."

"In our Basque language, we call them Pottoks. They are an ancient breed of pony with small, stocky bodies and large heads, very shy and apt to travel in small herds. The interesting thing about them is that they can predict the weather. When they feel bad weather coming, they break into small groups and move into the valleys. They reunite with the larger herd in the spring. In that way, they adapt to the changes in our climate. We believe they have lived in this region for centuries."

"I've seen this picture somewhere before."

"I'm not surprised. I sketched it from a postcard. It's a famous image that I've played with a bit. Perfect for your story, don't you think?"

As my story is all about shifting winds and separation, these horses are perfect.

Esteve has stayed out of his office to allow us time to talk, but now he must get some work done before it's time to join his family for dinner around ten PM. I'm still not used to long breaks during the day and the late-night meals. Alaya is conferring with Esteve about our choice. Her other sketches are also quite good. There is one of a flock of Latxa sheep walking a trail to the high country, with one ram looking back. Soulful brown eyes peer intensely out of a dark face framed by curling horns set off by white wool. He is staring into a horizon that is behind the viewer. But it's the drawing of the horses weathering separation with the hope of return that best captures my theme.

Alaya turns to me. "Would you like to come out to the farmhouse later this week? I'd like to introduce you to my husband and my children."

Knowing that Gibert has rounds, Esteve offers me the use of his car. My heart soars even as my stomach flip- flops. My work here is almost finished and I have decisions to make. What will I say to my mother? I don't want to be the one to tell her she has a twin sister who is alive and well. How will she feel about me if she finds out that I guessed she had not been an only child and then made up a story about it that turned out to be nearly true? Now I have to ask myself, how do I feel about having done that? Guilt eats at me as if I were a child who has spun elaborate stories to entertain her friends and then been caught by the truth.

What about Alaya? Apparently she's always known about having a twin, but she's never done anything about it. That's got to be as bad as what I've done. I've always hated secrets and here I am, caught in the mother of all secrets. Of course, this is not my only deception. Gibert doesn't know about Peter and Peter doesn't know about Gibert, so that's another decision I have to make. Do people keep secrets because they can't make decisions?

❧ Valerie ☙

13

ETXEA

*T*he farmhouse is nothing like I expected. I pictured Alaya living in a house about the size of
Lita's bungalow in Los Altos. Instead, the house is an
imposing two-story *caserío vasco* with an open trellis
of oak beams separated by brick and stone that looks
out at the barns and sheds that dot the property. The
outbuildings are spare of ornamentation save for iron
fittings and carved corbels that give the compound
the look of something old adapted for modern use.
This is a working farm reminiscent of a watercolor
I once saw where expansive grazing pastures and an
apple orchard washed across a canvas. Where the apples fell, industry sprouted in many different forms.

Alaya is out the door and down the porch steps
almost before I get out of the car. Along with a tour
of the grounds, I get a lesson in history, ecology, and
economics. Standing in the empty lambing barn, she
explains that the sheep are still in the high country.
They will come back in the late fall and the lambs will
be born in December and brought to tables in the
spring. The herd is mostly dairy sheep; she shows me

stacks of cheese rounds aging on shelves in another building, and an apple-cider operation in yet another building.

Inside the house, she introduces me to her husband, Elazar. He sits at a large plank table in the kitchen with papers and record books spread before him. We chat easily in Spanish about the house. He tells me that the farm belongs to Alaya's family and that the original house, built four hundred years ago, has been renovated many times to accommodate changes in fashion and use. He has just finished the latest renovation, bringing light through new windows into what was once a dark interior.

We leave Elazar to his paperwork, and Alaya settles me in the living room. She retrieves a large leather album from her desk and sets it in my lap with all the ceremony of a collector presenting an eager bibliophile with a cherished first edition.

"You know, twins run in families," she says, as I begin to leaf through the pages of photographs. "So I was not surprised when Domeka and Danel were born. They are ten years younger than you are, Valerie. Elazar and I married late and then we waited to have children. The boys are fifteen now. They're in school today, but they'll be home later so you can meet them."

Alaya goes to the kitchen while I leaf through the lives of these cousins I never knew I had. When she returns with two glasses of apple cider, I ask her why my grandfather never returned to the United States to look for his wife and daughter. Alaya gives me a history lesson instead of a satisfying answer.

"We Basques have a long history of exile and return. You discovered that when you researched your book. The Inquisition, the civil war, the world wars—we've always had to balance the preservation of our land and our culture with surviving the times. My father talked often of returning to America, but the decision was taken away from him. The American government came to feel that they had let too many Basque sheepherders into the country, and so they closed the doors to us."

Alaya paces. She seems to be choosing her words carefully. "Your book struck such a chord with me—exile and return. My boys were born right after the civil war, when the country was recovering from economic disaster. Some of the children who had been exiled for their safety returned to us. Others never did."

She folds her arms across her body in what strikes me as a protective gesture.

The emerging truth is competing with all the stories chattering in my head—my Lita and her Alonso; Alonso and Iban, the fictional sisters in my novel who I modeled after the real sisters Dolores and Alaya. There is so much I still don't understand, but the history Alaya offers is as good a place as any to begin sorting it all out. "But you stayed here through all that?"

"Yes. Even though the divided sympathies in Spain threatened us, we decided to stay on our farm. We survived the war the same way you did, because it wasn't fought on our land. My father died peacefully in his bed. He died in the land he loved." Alaya walks to the window and looks out over the vast landscape.

It's quite an empire he left her. "Why did your father go to the United States in the first place then?"

I set the photo album aside.

Alaya turns to face me. "I think in the United States there was much growth and opportunity."

Alaya takes a seat in a straight-back chair across from me and I have a déjà vu moment. An image of my straight-backed mother flashes into my mind, contrasting with my shorter and rounder figure. Slouched comfortably among the sofa pillows, I don't even try to match Alaya's posture.

"That is what attracted Iban and Alonso to your country. Here, we live as we always have, with political unrest that threatens us constantly. But it is a situation we understand. I think that Iban adapted well to his new country. He came to understand it and he profited from it. But Alonso was better suited to the rural life, where people travel ancient paths to desolate places and back again to rejoin the family."

This rolls around in my head for a moment. "He couldn't have done that in California? The Central Valley is pretty rural."

"No, Valerie. Here—the home, *etxea*—is the place we always come back to. Here, when we fight to keep our land, we fight a neighbor we know. In America, you fight people you don't know to keep your land. New industries destroy old paths before most people have a chance to adapt.

"In America, sheep herds number in the thousands, but most herders have no stake in the sheep or the land. Some who work for the boss make enough money to return to *etxea*. Others decide to stay. America is the land of opportunity for many. Here, fewer prosper, but those who do have a wealth in their land and culture that is not easily taken from them."

If only I had met Alaya before I finished my book. Will Esteve will allow me one more pass through the manuscript before it's released to the printer? Alaya is caught up in her story.

"My father had no love for the high country, but the months he spent up there gave him time to devise new ways of profiting from our land. The cheese and cider operations were his ideas. He turned the herding operation over to our cousins and we all benefited."

Something still sits wrong with me. "But how could he have left my mother and my grandmother like he did and never tried to see them again?"

Alaya sighs. She is silent, gathering her thoughts. "Valerie, I have asked myself that question. I don't have an answer. I think the real question you want to ask is why I have lived knowing that I have a twin sister and done nothing about it."

"Yes, that's my question."

Alaya remains seated in her beautifully rigid posture, as if she were a ballet dancer waiting for a musical cue to set her in motion. "I made a decision to follow the path that Alonso and Leora set. I could see no good that would come from disrupting your lives. My father was a disruption in your grandmother's life. She made a new life for your mother and herself. My father returned with me to an old way of life. It was their decision. What right did I have to change things?"

That sounds logical, but I still don't like it. "Well then, why did you arrange to meet me? The cat's out of the bag now."

"That's up to you."

"You mean you aren't willing to let my mother know about you, but you are willing to let *me* tell her?"

"Valerie, I don't mean to upset you. I'm not willing anything here. I was assigned to do the cover for your book. I recognized your name. I read your book and I could tell you knew something about our history. Then Esteve told me you were coming to Spain and suggested a meeting. I decided I wanted to meet you."

"What do you expect the outcome will be?" "I don't know."

I excuse myself to go to the bathroom. The face reflected in the mirror above the sink is not a happy face. What did I expect the outcome of this weekend would be? I thought it was all about getting answers to my questions. I never thought about what I'd have to do with the answers. I run water in the sink and splash it on my face. The best thing to do might be to stop asking questions. As quick as that thought forms in my head, another question banners across my brain.

I walk back out to the living room where Alaya is gathering our empty cider glasses. She's not looking happy either.

"Aunt Alaya, you haven't asked about Leora, your mother."

She lays the tray down and retakes her seat. Tears well up in her eyes, but just as quickly as they come, she turns them off. She is so like my mother.

"All I know about my mother is from letters Iban wrote and a few stories my father told. I know that she got a government job. I know that she never re-married, that she traveled a lot and that she raised your mother in many different cities. And I knew about you." She locks on to my eyes with her deep co-coa-colored eyes so characteristic of Basque people. I get goose bumps.

"My father always spoke kindly of her. He told me that she was pretty and fun, but that she was determined to get a bigger piece of the pie than most first-generation immigrants have a right to expect. He said that she was very ambitious and that he was wrong to marry her."

Alaya looks away. "You tell me about your grandmother."

Before I have time to think of what to say, the heavy front door flies open and the room is filled with noise. My teenage cousins roll into the room like half-grown sheepdogs on a tear. They introduce themselves, one speaking in Spanish, the other in English. This seems to be a game they've concocted and they are delighted with my ability to keep up with the thrust and parry. Their father appears at the entrance to the living room and gives them some instruction in still another language, Euskara I assume.

"We don't mean to be rude." Danel addresses me while throwing a punch at his brother.

"We are very pleased to make your acquaintance." Domeka ignores the assault and delivers a princely bow.

"We are very happy to have a girl cousin!" Danel grabs my hand and pulls me to my feet. The boys lead me outdoors where they demonstrate their prowess at handball against the side of the cider house. It is a welcome diversion.

Alaya announces dinner. The conversation around the table is about the boys' school activities and the sports they enjoy. They ask me questions about California. They want to know if I've ever met John Wayne, Marilyn Monroe, or Elvis Presley. I try to explain how big California is and that the stars live in the southern part of the state while I live in the north.

After dinner, the boys have chores and homework to do. What it would have been like to grow up with brothers or sisters? I pose this question to Alaya over coffee.

"Do you ever wonder what it would have been like to have grown up with a sister?"

"Yes, of course—especially when Papi was away for months. Papi told me about Dolores after I found one of Iban's letters. He told me that God gave him two girls, identical, like dolls cut from folded paper. He said that God split us apart because He wanted one of us to grow up in the old country and one of us to grow up in the new country. We would meet some-day, he said, and find the best of both worlds in each other.

"I often wondered what it would be like to grow up in a big city like Dolores did. When I went to art school in Barcelona, it was a bit like experiencing two versions of myself. I have always imagined the life Dolores lived compared with my life. I imagined her content in her world, as I have been in mine."

"My mother was less content than you imagined." These words slip out. It is a discussion I don't want to invite, so I ask her, "You never wanted to meet her?"

"It didn't seem possible. She was a shadow of a life I was born to but not destined to live." Alaya rose from the table and carried our coffee cups to the sink. Over her shoulder, she said in a low voice, "Papi gave your grandmother her choice, you know."

"What do you mean?"

"My mother chose to keep Dolores and send me away."

Back in my apartment in Barcelona, the awfulness of what Alaya has told me weighs heavy on my mind. It doesn't fit my memory of the grandmother who loved me so much. Alaya is so matter-of-fact about what happened, so unconcerned about setting things right. She doesn't seem bitter, but there is a cold edge to her— except when her sons are present. She does seem pleased at how they respond to me, and I to them. Before I left, they made me promise I would write to them and send them photographs of California.

"Take pictures of Stanford."

"And the Golden Gate Bridge and the Pacific Ocean."

"Take pictures of California girls." They poked each other. "And of your boyfriends, and we'll tell you if we approve."

As Alaya walked me out to the car, she said, "Are you going to tell her about me?"

I don't know. Did Alaya make the right decisions? I can't say. I do know that I will make different decisions. I am mulling that over on a Monday morning, walking past the plaza on my way to Esteve's office, when a disheveled young man runs smack into me, catching my shoulder with his. The impact spins me around and knocks me off the short curb, into the cobbled street. Trying to stay upright, my foot lands close to an open drain and when I finally lose my balance and go down, my ankle gives way and jams my foot down into the abyss. It feels like a demon from deep under the earth has clamped its teeth on my foot, keeping me tethered while I try to pull away. And that was probably a mistake. I hear something snap and feel an intense burning sting in my ankle. The young man stoops over me, to comfort me I think, but no. He pulls my purse from underneath me, where I have fallen on it, and takes off running! It all happens so fast that people walking by see only a girl laying in the street. If anyone notices the purse snatcher, they don't react. A businessman stoops down to see if I'm okay. I'm not. Black spots float in front of my eyes, and the world goes dark.

When I come to a few seconds later, I'm still sprawled in the street and I can't get up. I try to float my thoughts above the pain. Someone says, "She's in shock."

The next time I wake up, I am in a hospital, in a surgical recovery unit, with a cast on my leg that runs clear to my hip.

I'm so drugged, I think pleasantly about the items in my purse that I will never see again—my passport, my identification, my travelers checks, my favorite lipstick. Then I think about what I didn't have in my purse—my manuscript, my address book, my engagement ring from Peter. As groggy as I am, I am having my first moment of clarity since I left California. I actually let Peter give me an engagement ring before I left for Spain knowing that I wasn't sure this was what I wanted. Before meeting my mother for lunch, I took the ring off my finger and put it in my coin purse. I told myself it was because I wasn't ready to tell anyone yet. I guess it makes sense. He is graduating this year and I'm twenty-five years old. Most of my girlfriends are already married, which is why I spend so much time with the undergraduates I teach.

I'm going to have a lot of time to think about this. Gibert has been by to see me. I've sustained the unlucky kind of break in my ankle that will keep me in some kind of a cast for months.

A hospital volunteer arrives with a vase of flowers. They are from Peter. Phone calls have been made and the word is getting out. The card on the flowers informs me in the flowing script of a florist's pen that Peter is flying to Spain this weekend to see "his girl." Gibert stops by my room once again. This time he has a telegram.

WHAT CAN WE DO TO GET YOU HOME? MOTHER.

I'm calculating how fast and how far away I might be able to get on crutches when the nurse brings me drugs that make me pass out and sleep for eighteen hours.

❧ *Dolores* ❧

14

SMOKE

*V*alerie is in the hospital in Spain. A Señor Borrell
called to tell me she's been the victim of a mugger,
a thug who stole her purse and broke her ankle in the
process. She won't be coming home anytime soon,
Borrell told me, but she's doing well under the care of
a doctor who happens to be his son. And Señor Borrell happens to be the owner of the publishing house
that is publishing her book. Is that what they call a
thesis these days? This is confusing, but I know better
than to try to sort out Valerie's affairs. I'll tackle the
part I can do something about.

I make phone calls to see what I can do from here
to help Valerie re-establish her identity. The most I
can manage is to assemble a package of forms and
phone numbers that will help her get new papers.

The next thing I know, Peter is at my door. He has
been stopping by regularly. At first, I thought of him
as if he were a neighbor's puppy who hangs around,
waiting to be liked. But he's grown on me. His family is from Ohio, he tells me. He's trying to decide
whether to give a career in baseball a whirl or begin

law school. I ask him if his folks have an opinion on
that, and he rolls his eyes. He asks me what I think. I
surprise myself by telling him law school will always
be there, but the time he can play baseball will probably be short.

We talk about a player's life—starting in the mi-
nors, traveling, hoping the seasons of living on nothing will pay off. I entertain his fantasy from the point
of view of one who gave up her own.

Today he's come to tell me he is going to fly to
Spain to make sure Valerie is okay. I ask him if she
wants him to do that. Doesn't matter, he says, he's
going. He doesn't like the idea of her being laid up
and alone. Something about the solicitous tone in
Señor Borrell's voice when he called told me that Valerie is receiving plenty of attention. Hopefully this
young man is not going to get his heart broken.

I put Peter out of my mind. I have my own heart to
think about. Four months have flown by since my
weekend in Bakersfield. Of course, I confronted Iban
about the twin sister I didn't know I had. I still don't
think I got the straight story, but it seems that, yes, I
was born a twin, but that my sister didn't live much
past a year. Of everything he told me, he seemed most
uncomfortable with that little detail. It does explain
the two urns that wait in the columbarium. Perhaps
Leora planned to unite her little family in death. Who
would know where my sister's ashes are?

I did wrestle my twin sister's name out of the old
man—Alaya. It means joyful. The joyful one died and
the sorrowful one—me—lived.

Since I've been back from Bakersfield, I've been
immersed in creating collages. Roger and I still see

each other, but not as much as before. I tramp around on the trails off Skyline Road and practice using my camera. Roger helped me turn the closet in my sitting room into a darkroom. Since it's right next to the bathroom, he was able to pipe water into the closet for the chemical baths I use to develop my photos. He figured out how to ventilate the room without bringing in light so I don't pass out; it's such a small space. My house is becoming as much a collage as the creations I produce.

In my darkroom, I enlarge the photos I take of oak, olive, fig, and pepper trees. I cut them into pieces and arrange them into portraits, along with pieces I cut from the small collection of Leora's photos. In one piece, Leora emerges from the spine of an oak tree, her many-eyed expressions among the leaves, some clinging to branches, others piled at the roots of the tree. In another piece, I've broken down her glamorous friends and pieced them back together with fig-leaf shoulders and pepper-tree hair. They look like stylish wood sprites or a coven of playful friends. I experiment with the exposure to get sharply focused branches or sepia-toned leaves. It is tedious, exhilarating work that totally absorbs me.

The more I work with the pieces of Leora's life, pulling things apart and piecing them back together, the more I see her layers of contradiction. She was at once an observer of life who drew people in and an inscrutable keeper of secrets, other people's as well as her own. That's why she was valued as a court reporter.

She didn't take all those secrets to the grave though. Digging through her Vuitton steamer trunk one afternoon, I unearthed a trove of stories she wrote. They must have been based on some of the more notorious cases she recorded.

Back in my studio, I use a razor blade to cut and lift typed phrases from the yellowed paper and add them to my collages.

In Leora's writing, I see her humor, moral implacability, professional grit, and feminine wile. It provides another layer in the archeology of my creation. Along with the quotes from her stories, I pull apart her jewelry and add the pieces to my collages— an enamel cat face among the eyes in the oak tree, feathers from a brooch on the tree sprites, fiery opals around the witch women.

Weirdly beautiful." Laura sits cross-legged on the floor in my studio leafing through my growing portfolio. She is getting quite proficient on my piano, so much so that I paid to have it tuned. She keeps after me about the Wednesday bridge club.

"Dee, there's a reason I want you to do this. Marianne Watson plays with us."

"Who is that?" I'm not really listening. I'm sitting on the floor, fingering through a box of old earrings, sorting out the ones I want to keep for their stones.

"Don't you read the *Town Crier*?"

"Sometimes. What is she, a columnist?

"She owns the Main Street Art Co-op."

"Oh." I'm still not getting it.

Laura scoots over closer to me. "Dee, you need to show your art. You need to start getting your collages out there for people to see."

There is more to Laura than I realized.

❧ *Dolores* ❧

15

MIRRORS

Once again, Father Mike and I sit in his office after vespers. I try to attend either the quiet early Friday evening service or the Sunday worship every week. With everything else in my life so unsettled, Jesus'words *Come unto me all ye that labour and are heavy laden and I will give you rest* are salve.

"You are coming up on an anniversary. It's been just about a year since your mother passed away. How are you feeling?"

"My life has changed a lot."

"Yes, it has—new work, new people in your life—a lot of change." Father Mike leans back in his chair. The chair squeaks and groans. He clasps his hands behind his head in a gesture I know well. He's about to challenge me. "What hasn't changed?"

I roll my eyes to heaven and set my chin on my folded hands. Silence enters the room from a high window in the rectory and sits down in a corner. The wall clock beats with a somnolent rhythm. Frogs and crickets are tuning up for the evening symphony outside.

When I open my mouth to speak, words tumble over my tongue like creek water washing the silt off rocks. "I still feel like there is a missing piece. It's like I'm hanging out here by myself, like I've been left. It's not just that Henry and my mother are gone. I feel a deep sadness that a father and a sister I never knew are gone too. Valerie is gone. Maybe she'll decide to stay in Spain. Maybe she'll return to Stanford and become a professor. Maybe she'll marry Peter and there will be grandchildren, but I don't see that happening. How did I end up with no family?"

"You have an uncle."

Warm liquid spills into my eyes. "Going to see Uncle Iban was like seeing a light coming from underneath a closed door. It's like a light in a closet that gets left on and you think maybe there is something there, but when you look, there is nothing."

I open my purse and pull out a tissue to catch the overflow of disappointment I have dammed up inside me.

"Dee, what did your uncle tell you about your twin sister?"

We've talked about this before. "He just said we lost her after our first birthday."

"That sounds like a man choosing his words very carefully. Did you ask any questions?"

"No. I was just so mad at my mother for keeping all this from me and for letting me believe my father had abandoned us."

"You know, you found a whole community of people there who knew about you. Is that maybe a family of sorts?"

"I thought about that. I wanted to feel a connection to them, but I didn't."

"Connections need to be nurtured. Keep that door open." Then he leaned forward and put his elbows on the desk between us. "How are things going with Roger?"

"Oh, well, that's a light that's gone out too. I mean, we are very good friends. We spend a fair amount of time together, but the romance kind of dried up after we got back from Bakersfield. I think it didn't go quite the way he hoped it would."

"Because?"

"Okay, because I pushed him away. I've been alone for so long. Even when Henry was alive, we lived apart most of our lives because of the Army. I don't think I really know how to be close to someone."

"Because of the Army?"

"You don't quit, do you, Father." The direction of this conversation is very uncomfortable. "Okay, the truth is, I followed Leora from city to city when I was growing up, and then I married a man who expected me to follow him from Army post to Army post. I said no."

"In that way you were like Leora."

"What?"

"Well, Leora told your father she wouldn't follow him."

"And I repeated that pattern in my marriage. I see what you're getting at. I don't like it, but I see it."

"Often the people we are most angry with are mirrors of our own souls."

Father Mike lifts himself out of his chair and reaches for his Bible and his appointment book. I stand up and follow behind as he turns out the lights and locks the doors. He puts a companionable arm across my shoulder as he walks me to my car.

"You know, Dee, if you don't want to be alone, you may have to open a door and turn on a light."

❧ Dolores ❧

16

FIRE

I drive through the hills on my way home. The sun is setting earlier these days and change is in the air. A season is passing. Something is coming and something is going. How much say do I have in what gets left behind and what takes its place?

In my collages, each step in the process alters the character of the piece. Cut too much away and context has no power to help define the theme. Allow too much in and . . .

I turn the car into the lane. Flashing red lights shoot like sparklers in the night sky. The air is thick and glowing above the rotating lights. In the dim light, shadowy figures appear to stand in the middle of the street. Those are people and that is my house they are standing in front of!

This can't be happening. It's as if someone has turned on the lights in my head one sense at a time. The acrid odor of smoke fills my nostrils. The old wood house is erupting like a fall bonfire. Whistles and cracks of flames deafen me. I throw the car into park in the middle of the street and jump out, not bothering to cut the ignition. I stand in the street with my neighbors, completely stunned.

My pepper tree looks like the burning corpse of a woman with her hair on fire. The back part of my house is black and chewed, its bony skeleton exposed. The front of my house chokes in the smoke, trying to live but losing the battle. A few firemen shoot water into the savage blaze from the ground, while others stand on the rooftops of my neighbors' homes, watering down everything in the path of the fire. A fireman appears in front of me.

"Is this your house?"

"Yes, this is my home."

"Your neighbors said you live here alone."

"Yes, is that important?"

"No one was in the house, then?"

"No, no one. Just everything I own in the world, but no people."

"Ma'am, I'm sorry to tell you this, but the house is a total loss. At this point we are working to save your neighbors' houses."

I am glued to the spot. I have no feeling in my body anywhere. Conversation around me blends into the crackle and pop of the flames that have spent most of their rage. The fire seems content to burn my house peacefully to embers now.

"How did this happen?" I run through the possibilities in my mind. Did I leave something burning on the stove? Was there something flammable in my art supplies? Was there a gas leak and an explosion? Was someone burning leaves that caught a breeze and set fire to my roof?

"We haven't determined a cause. There will be an investigation, but there are two likely scenarios. Bad wiring—these houses were built in the twenties with substandard wiring. And arson."

"You think someone set fire to my house deliberately?"

"Ma'am, I did not say that. We do know that an arsonist has been at work in the hills this past summer. Usually it's a kid, and it usually stops when school starts again, but we'll investigate. We'll find the cause."

I start to shiver. Laura comes up behind me with a sweater she pulled from my car when she turned the engine off. She wraps it around my shoulders and brushes my hair off my face.

"Dee, I'm so sorry." We both burst into tears.

My other neighbors are busy keeping their children at bay or hosing down their fences and rooftops. My house is gone now. It looks like the Wicked Witch of the West in *The Wizard of Oz*, a solitary hat sitting among steaming remains. The thing that has remained amazingly intact is the piano, probably the one item I cared least about.

My practical mind tries to minimize the psychological damage. Clothes? I can buy more. Furniture? I didn't have much, nothing I cared about. I'll miss the davenport. My collages! My collection of what Leora treasured—this loss punches me in the stomach. As if she can see this blow, Laura pulls me away from the commotion.

"Dee!" Laura puts both her hands on my shoulders and forces me to look at her. My eyes are burning with smoke and tears. "Dee, listen to me. Your neighbors tried to save your house but it went up so quickly. While the others were scrambling for hoses, before the fire department got here, I ran into your studio and pulled out as much as I could. Your collages, your camera, and a few small boxes of stuff you had in your studio are safe at my house. But then there was an explosion."

"You shouldn't have done that Laura! You risked your life going into a burning house!"

But her words are like a life ring tossed in a black sea, a speck of brightness. The last word she said finally makes an impact: Explosion. My darkroom. Could the chemicals in my darkroom have caused the fire? If I caused this fire out of ignorance, then I deserve to lose my home. Stupid! How could I be so careless and stupid? Laura has the clairvoyance of a medium and the compassion of a saint. I'm sure I did not utter this thought out loud, but her next words are, "No one deserves to have this happen, Dee, least of all you. This is just the most awful thing. It could happen to any one of us. I am so sorry it happened to you."

Then she looks down the street in the direction of her house. As if she's putting a toe in treacherous waters, she draws into herself and her next words are less confident.

"Dee, I'd like to offer to have you stay at our house. Lord knows we have the room. But the truth is, Fred is a bit of a stick. He has a routine and he doesn't like to have it disturbed."

It suddenly occurs to me that there may be a reason that Laura spends so much time at my house. What does it say about me that I've never even thought about that?

She stands up a little straighter. "But I have a plan."

Part 2

THE HEART'S HIGH PLACE

❧ Valerie ❧

17

ROOTS

I'm not taking the Borrells up on their invitation to recuperate at their home. I'm not lying here in this hospital bed waiting for Gibert and Peter to meet over my inert body either. The most sensible thing I can do is call Aunt Alaya.

When Elazar comes to collect me, he's driving a gull-wing Mercedes 300SL. He pulls the passenger seat all the way back and guides my leg that is mummified in plaster to rest on the dashboard while I squat down on my other leg looking like I'm trying to pee in the gutter. I do a chicken dance to lower myself down into the seat and pull my other leg in. It's a good thing I'm a stretchy sort.

"I'm sorry, Valerie, the boys took the truck earlier this morning to repair some fences and the Land Rover was out of gas."

We are outside Barcelona now, zipping around the curves in the road at high speed. It's good medicine. All the blood rushes to my heart, dulling the pain in my leg. I'm curious about how a farmer came to drive such a cool car and I'm bold enough to ask.

"Ah, well." Elazar's eyes crinkle with pleasure. "This was a gift from a generous sponsor."

It turns out that Uncle Elazar is a national handball champion. Now that's the first thing I would have mentioned, but in this family we are tight-lipped. We don't even leave crumbs on the trail. That sounds like a theme for my next novel.

Back at the farmhouse, Alaya has a spacious room behind the kitchen set up for me where I can close the door and rest or keep it open and be part of the action.

Alaya helps me up into the bed and positions my leg on some pillows. Then she brings me a glass of water so I can take my pain pill.

"Doctor's orders," she says with a wink. "Doctor Gibert Borrell." She practically sings his name.

I guess it's time for a talk. I have to talk this out with someone because I've come up with nothing trying to figure it out on my own. I explain my dilemma.

Alaya is a careful listener. She doesn't speak right away, but when she does, it's a divination.

"What are you trying to choose between—two men or two lives?"

Alaya walks to the window and looks out over her estate. The sheep have returned. We can see them grazing in the distant pastures. Farm workers are lugging baskets of apples from the orchard to the cider house. The cycle of activity in this place is like the blood in our veins, nourishing and ever present even if it goes unnoticed. You would notice it only if it stopped. She turns back to me and leans against the window frame, her arms folded across her chest.

"I chose a life. Let me tell you about that." The sun coming in the window plays on her face and I can see memories warm the depth of her dark eyes.

"In 1933 I had a chance to leave Navarre. Many Basque people were fleeing the political unrest. I could not go to the United States because your borders had been closed to us, this time under the National Origins Act. But I had another option. I was in love with the younger son of a shipping tycoon. You've heard of the Aboitiz shipping line?"

I shake my head no.

"Well, the Aboitiz family went to the Philippines. They've done well there. In our culture, though, younger sons must find another line of work. They don't inherit the family business. Luis wanted to go to California. He figured that the borders would not be closed forever, so he decided to get as close to the United States as he could. He chose Baja California.

"Papito told me to go. 'Go with Luis. He will get rich in America,' he said to me. 'Find your sister. Iban will help you. When your husband gets rich, you can come back to the farm. It will be here for you.'

"It was clear to me that if I married Luis, we would establish our lives in a new country. I didn't doubt that he would make good, and he has. He is still in Baja California, in Ensenada. I knew I had a community to go to in Bakersfield. I even knew that Dolores was in San Francisco, that she'd married your father and had a baby girl—you."

"How did you know all that?"

"Every large Basque community, wherever it is located—Argentina, Mexico, Canada, even the Soviet Union—has a mutual-aid society that is as much about passing information on dispersed families' whereabouts as it is about collecting money to help displaced people. Word about where my mother was got back to us. She made a bit of a name for herself as the first female court reporter in the West. Knowing where Leora was made it easy to keep track of my sister."

"But you decided not to go see her."

"I decided that my roots were here and here I would stay. I did not have a burning desire to get rich. Like my father, I love this land. From the way Papito described California—so spread out, so many people coming and going—I did not think I would love it."

"And Luis?"

"Apparently I did not love him enough. I have no regrets."

The pills are fogging my anxiety and replacing it with light-headed euphoria. I work to keep my focus on the tale of star-crossed lovers. It's as if my soul were divided into one part happy child hearing a love story and one part suspicious seeker of the truth. Alaya continues her story.

"I met Elazar a year later. He was very different from Luis, but there were similarities. Elazar is competitive and adventurous but not a wanderer. He's a hard worker. He helped me build what we have today, a family business to pass on to our boys if they want it. It's not an international shipping business, but it's enough. And Elazar, he's handsome, don't you think?"

She laughs and then turns to raise the window. A fresh, apple-scented breeze blows in.

"So, you don't think there is a 'right one'?"

"No, I don't."

I don't hear anything after that.

I am wandering somewhere between sleep and awareness. Do roots matter to me? Apparently they did not matter to Lita. I am getting to know a lot about the Basque side of my family. I know nothing about my grandmother's Greek immigrant family. And my dad's people, who were they? The faces of an old couple living in an apartment somewhere drift by. They are dead. They came from somewhere and went somewhere. I sink back into sleep and bob up again later with this thought in my head: people are like the irises in my mother's garden. They form rhizomes that creep through the dirt and shoot roots everywhere. If they get cut off, they keep growing. If they aren't separated, they sometimes weaken and die.

We come from good stock, my Lita used to say. She cut herself off from her roots, and strong, capable women blossomed from her stock. Alaya chose to stay clumped together with her family, tangled in a showy display in her homeland. I can't see that this has weakened her though, so my metaphor fizzles. All I know in this present moment is that Alaya is right. I have to decide whether to choose a man or a life.

❧ Valerie ❧

17

CHOICES

Two days later, I'm feeling more myself. I'm sitting up in my room, listening to the rain drumming on the tile roof. My hair is drying after a much needed shampooing and I'm reading the last of John Dos Passos's U.S.A. trilogy, *The Big Money*. Good thing I'm up because Alaya walks into the room with a cheery greeting. "You've got visitors."

All my senses perk up as if I were a small animal sensing danger. Pant legs rustle in the next room. The floorboards shiver from the tread of big feet. I inhale the scent of wet wool, musk, and hair oil. Touching my fingers to my throat, I emit a squeak of alarm as Gibert and Peter walk through the door. Gibert interprets this as a squeal of delight. He strides across the room, bends over me, and gives me a kiss.

"How's my patient? I've brought you a friend."

Gibert squats down in front of me and takes my hand, feeling for my pulse, which is racing. This gives me a clear shot of Peter, who is standing back with a wry smile on his face.

"Hello, Valerie." He says this in an upbeat way with an undertone that could be saying *Well, isn't this interesting?* Or *You hussy!* Or *Would have been nice if you'd let me know we were over.*

Alaya leans against the doorframe looking amused. As soon as I catch her eye, she turns on her heel and heads back into the kitchen. "You young people visit while I fix some hot apple cider."

Elazar comes in and out of the room carrying chairs for the men to sit on. Gibert sits on the one Elazar has placed next to my bed and Peter pulls his chair around to face me.

I read somewhere that one of the saints—Ezekiel, I think—was transported directly into heaven by God. I wish for that. Of course, heaven would probably not be my destination. There is probably a special hell for women who play men for fools.

Peter leans back in his chair, crosses a leg over a knee, folds his arms over his chest, and watches as Gibert pulls a stethoscope out of his bag, slips it beneath my gown and prepares to listen to my heartbeat.

"Your pulse rate is pretty high, young lady."

I'm scrambling for words when Gibert finishes his examination, repacks his bag, and says, "Well, your friend has come a long way to see you, Valerie, and I'm due back at the hospital this afternoon, so I'm going to leave the two of you to visit. You seem to be doing well. The elevated heart rate is the result of a surprise visit from two admirers, am I right?"

"Oh, absolutely," I burble. Gibert kisses me again, pats my shoulder in a see-you-soon gesture, and goes out the door.

The survival instinct of the human species motivates all kinds of craziness. Maybe I will be able to keep these relationships separate and intact, at least until I can extricate myself in such a way that allows us all to keep our dignity. Then I follow Peter's gaze to the bare third finger of my left hand. I don't know what Gibert has told him or how much he has guessed, but it takes no genius to know the jig is up. I am guilty as charged, and Peter is probably just waiting for me to stop dancing at the end of my rope, give him back his ring, and let him sail on into other ports.

I open my mouth to begin an explanation, not knowing what words will tumble out, when Peter gets up, sits in the chair Gibert has just left, and gathers me into his arms. He crushes me to him, stroking his fingers up the back of my neck and pulling them back down through my damp hair. For one panicked moment I think *He's going to break my neck*, but the movement softens into one of comfort as he whispers, "I'm so sorry you've been hurt."

What is he talking about? My broken ankle? Gibert? Is Gibert seeing someone else? Is he talking about himself? Has he . . .

Peter pulls away, holding both my shoulders, and looks at me sternly. "I know we have a lot of talking to do, but remember this, Valerie. I love you."

Then he kisses me full on and gently holds me as if I were a wounded animal. I don't know how much he knows about what I've been up to over here, but apparently he plans to forgive me. How do I feel about this plan? We can't just pretend nothing has happened. Now I'm starting to get a little miffed. He's treating me as if I were some kind of prize that he has won.

I have to admit that it feels good to be in his arms again. As lovely and sophisticated a man as Gibert is,

I never really know where I stand with him. When we're together, he is a loving and devoted companion. When we're apart, which is most of the time, I tell myself he is completely absorbed in his work. I've ignored the clues: the broken dates he attributes to schedule changes, his apartment I've never seen, his friends I've never met. Truth is, Gibert is a sexy, companionable diversion, an arrangement his parents made hoping it might settle down their playboy son. An American girl from Stanford might open some doors for a talented, ambitious second son. Okay, that's just cynical; the Borrells have been nothing but nice to me.

Peter gives my shoulders a little shake and says, "Let's get you better and get you home."

Peter can only stay a few days. He has to get back to Stanford to finish up the fall term. I fill him in on Alaya and her family and extract a promise that he will not tell my mother. I should be in a shorter cast by Christmas, I tell him. I can travel then. I'll be back at Stanford in January. In the meantime, I'll stay here in the Basque countryside, scribbling away on a proposal for a dissertation on immigration themes in Spanish literature and plotting my next novel. Peter seems okay with that.

"I have something to talk to you about," he says, "but it can wait until you get home."

Peter declines Alaya's invitation to stay at the farmhouse. He wants to do some sightseeing, he says. Elazar offers him the use of his truck to knock around in and that's a perfect plan. It will give me time to think.

It's funny how having your leg stuck in a cast can sharpen your resolve to get moving. As much as I love the bustle of Barcelona and the peace and beauty of the Basque countryside, I know now that this is not my place. I'm a person compelled by ideas. I want to study how the movement of people contributes to the growth of nations and ultimately the world. What must be preserved? What has to die? Do old paths still provide a useful surface, like the paths the sheep have walked for generations, or should the path be changed and be lost? What do we fight for? What do we yield to?

Regardless of what new paths I forge, I won't make my grandmother's mistake. I don't want to break connections with my ethnic past. I will come back to this place as often as I can to dip my ladle into the cultural stew that sustains the Basque people all over the world. But live here? Europe is like an old bull running through the same streets, recovering from old injuries even as it fields new jabs to its vitals.

I won't make Alaya's mistake either. I don't want only the pastures I can see to be my borders. California is big and bold, and its enterprising spirit is in my blood. Palo Alto and the sleepy towns around it percolate with new ideas that promise to cut new paths in every field. It will start at Stanford and Berkeley.

I don't know what is coming, but the energy is palpable. Back home, when I walk through the neighborhoods and smell the sweet aroma of apricots and Italian plums mixed with the sharp scent of freshly planed wood stacked at new home sites, I see The Valley of the Heart's Delight making room for all comers.

The itch I have is not only in my leg, it's coursing through my whole body. I have a little money from Leora coming to me and a modest advance from my publisher put away for a rainy day. I'll apply for another grant. I'll give up my pricey student apartment on campus and find a cheap room to rent. If I get through my PhD program, I'll be able to supplement my writing income with a good teaching job. One thing for sure, come January I plan to be off my mother's payroll, paying my own way entirely.

I'm not the only one making plans. When Peter returns from his travels in Elazar's truck, he tells me he has decided to postpone law school and try out for a major league baseball team.

In the life I dreamed about with Peter, a Spanish literature professor and an attorney fit the picture perfectly. Easy to tuck a couple of kids into that album too. While life in bustling Barcelona or on a farm in the Basque land holds some appeal for me, it's family life that fills a hole in me I didn't know I had. The time I've spent with the Borrell family and with my aunt, uncle, and cousins has been a revelation. I grew up lonely, with only myself to watch after while my mother worked. Being part of a family is exhilarating. There is laughter, argument, negotiation, heaps of encouragement, showing off and holding forth, teasing and tussling, admonishment and advice—a daily human interaction I've never experienced in such intensity. All this passes before my eyes as Peter outlines the next few years of his life.

While Peter chatters on, I am weighing the options. My head tells me that the union of a professor and an attorney would produce a suitable environment for a family, but a professor and a baseball player—how would that work?

Peter and I sit in the kitchen late into the night discussing likely scenarios and in the end I give him back his ring. I cry. He has tears in his eyes too. We agree that we love and care for each other, but that the life of a rookie baseball player has no room for a young family. It's a short career, and when it's over, he hopes I will be there waiting for him.

When it's over, my heart tells me, I will be too old and too established in my career to start a family. If his plans work out, he'll be in a perfect place to marry and have kids—just not with me.

Elazar drives Peter to the airport in Barcelona at dawn for the long flight home. Alaya wanders into the kitchen in her bathrobe and makes us coffee. I have an awful headache from being up half the night and then crying into my pillow. Now I'm back at the kitchen table. My mouth is cotton, my heart has a stiletto stuck in it, and my stomach is empty and sick.

My aunt sets a cup of coffee in front of me. The roasty aroma promises comfort, but when I stare into the black liquid in the cup, it triggers a surprising reaction. I struggle to my feet, tuck my crutch under my arm, and pick up the cup with my other hand.

"Alaya, you and my mother are going to have to work out your relationship yourselves—or not. I can't fix this." And I hobble back to my room, swinging the door closed behind me with the tip of my crutch.

❧ Dolores ☙

19

REBUILDING

*A*n enterprising Laura outlines her outrageous plan like a fast-talking used-car salesman.

"You know Marianne Watson, the one I told you about who owns the art co-op in the village? Well, she lives on an estate in the hills that has a little cottage around back. I know for a fact that no one is using that cottage right now."

Her mouth is moving, but I can't make sense of what she is saying. Is she suggesting I break into this woman's guesthouse and camp out?

"After the fire chief declared your house a total loss—before you got here—I went home and called Marianne. I knew you would need a place to stay for several months and Marianne said yes, and she's getting it ready for you right now. You can move in tonight."

"I can't do that! I don't even know her!"

"What does that matter? Trust me, she is a wonderful person. You'll have a place to stay that will give you privacy while you sort this all out. It's perfect."

I glare at Laura without an ounce of thankfulness in my bones.

"You have nowhere else to go." She puts her hands on her hips, narrows her green cat eyes at me, and sets her lips in a firm line.

She has me there.

"You have nothing to lose."

Right again. I have nothing else in this world to lose. God has stripped me of everything and dropped me down a well. I can't just huddle up in the darkness and cold and let the Ishmaelites come by and cart me off. How strange that this Bible story is in my head; I must have been paying more attention in church than I realized. But truly, this latest loss is of biblical proportions, at least to me. I make a mental note to look up the story of Joseph and see how it ends.

After I give my new address to the fire chief, I get in my car and follow Laura's car as it winds through the hills. We drive over a stone bridge that crosses the creek and through a large iron gate that has been left open. The house isn't visible from the road. We continue winding through acres of landscape that I can't fully appreciate in the dark. When we crest the hill, the house is shining in the light of a three-quarter moon. It is a low Spanish Mission-style house with a red tiled roof embracing an expansive courtyard that has an intricately tiled fountain in the center. The fountain burbles in low tones like the steady purr of a sleepy cat. Laura stops her car, gets out, and walks over to my open window.

"Marianne said she'd leave the key under the door mat of the guest cottage. She'll come and introduce herself in the morning. Just drive around the back of the house and you'll see the cottage beyond the rose garden." Then she opens the back door of my car and puts a small valise on the seat. "Here, I packed a nightgown and some toiletries for tonight, and pants and a sweater for tomorrow. We're about the same size, I think. I'll pick you up tomorrow and we'll go clothes shopping."

If I looked up *thoughtful* in the dictionary, I'm sure the definition would be *Laura McMillan*. I get out of the car and give her a hug.

This isn't a cottage, it's more like a villa. A small porch light burns next to a painted blue door nestled in the thick stucco walls. I retrieve the key and open the door. The familiar evening cacophony of crickets and frogs comforts me. My body is as weary as if I'd traveled the ocean to get here. Laura is right. What else could I have done? Drag myself over to El Camino Highway to look for a motel?

Marianne has left a brightly painted bowl full of fresh fruit and a plate of cinnamon cookies on the low Mission-style table. A flowered ceramic pitcher of cold water sits on the table next to a heavy stemmed glass. I am so thirsty I drink several glasses of water. I pop a cookie into my mouth, grab an apple, and wander into the bedroom. There's a cozy double bed with a white chenille bedspread and several pillows in red, orange, and pink. A high dresser, a wooden desk and chair, and a red leather love seat and ottoman draped with a Mexican blanket furnish the room. I fall on the bed fully clothed and sleep the sleep of the dead.

The next few days are a blur of activity. I suspect that Laura and Marianne have conspired to keep me so busy that I will not have time to grieve. Marianne is what I would have called a Los Altos matron if it weren't for her offbeat bohemian manner. She raised four perfect children—the boys are successful in their careers and the girls are happy in their homes in the new suburban communities that dot the foothills, raising beautiful sons and daughters of their own. Marianne's physician husband has cut his plastic-surgery practice back to three days a week so he can play golf and tend a small vineyard on their property. This leaves Marianne free to nurture the artists who show their work at her art co-op on Main Street. She has collected watercolors, acrylics, mosaics, sculpture, fabric art, jewelry, and pottery—but no collages yet, she says, sneaking a sly look at me from the corners of her perfectly made-up hazel eyes. She has waist-length honey-colored hair pulled into a low hanging ripple that she tied with a bright chiffon scarf. She wears long cotton Mexican skirts, peasant blouses, and espadrilles. She herself is a work of art, untouched by Dr. Watson's face-sculpting talents. Fine lines frame her knowing smile, adding substance to what may once have been just a pretty face.

Marianne has an ability to make everyone comfortable. She encourages the odd young novice with natural but unschooled talent and the housewife who creates jewelry while her toddlers nap. Older townspeople who have studied painting for years need only to have an eye for the unusual subject or unique perspective to be invited to join her merry band. She's even introduced some pieces to her gallery that she calls "modern." People actually come down all the way from the city to see her collection of Saul Salinsky's tangled cubes of color.

Marianne keeps an office above the gallery and rents out studio space. I plan to talk to her about setting up a darkroom there, but I will wait until I get the fire marshal's report on what caused my house to burn down.

Father Mike has heard about the fire and tracked me down to my casita in the hills.

"What will you do?" He's not employing his usual Socratic method of examination.

I surprise both of us when I find the answer. "I have insurance. I have to wait for the incident and inspection reports before I file. But I think I will have some options. I can rebuild to suit myself; I can rebuild to sell; or I suppose I could just clean up the lot and sell it." We sit beside the fountain and I trail my fingers in the water. "I have to decide what I want to do with my life. I have no husband, no job, and now I have no home. I have no moorings, no tethers."

"This is good?"

Ah, there is the Father Mike I know and love, always with the questions. "I have friends. I have interests. I will even say I have talents."

We sit shoulder to shoulder, looking out across an expanse of freshly cut grass toward the vineyard with its neatly trimmed vines. The air smells like honeysuckle, unusual for this late in the fall. He picks up my hand and holds it in his own. "What about love?"

"Believe it or not, I take your point." I think about Laura, who thrust herself into my life. Laura encouraged me and introduced me to Marianne. She made things happen for me. But she is hiding something and I haven't taken the time to find out what that is. And Roger; I'm sure he wonders why I cooled towards him, with no explanation, after we got back from Bakersfield. My face burns as I confess that I haven't been a very good friend.

Mike places my hand back in my lap. "What do you believe about your talent?"

"That I need to pursue it. That it's the hardest work I have ever done or ever will do."

"Harder than raising a daughter? Harder than being a daughter?"

"No."

"Pursue your talent Dee, but do not neglect love." He leans toward me and pats my hand again. "I have another spiritual exercise for you, Dee. Practice the First Corinthians kind of love that Saint Paul tells us is the most excellent way. We've been reading about that. It's the love that bears all things, believes all things, hopes all things, endures all things, and never ends. Pray for wisdom to know how to do that with your friends and your family."

"My family? You mean Valerie?"

"No, I mean your family, the living and the dead. Leora is gone from sight, but not from memory. And according to our faith, you will see her again. Let the Holy Spirit soften your heart toward your mother. It will do you good."

Father Mike shuffles his feet on the tile and we sit in silence for a moment. Smoke from a pile of leaves someone is burning in the distance wafts by. He sneezes, pulls a handkerchief from his pocket, and blows his nose with a mighty force. Then he raises a finger in the air and turns to address me.

"Daughter, give your art to the world with love and abandon." He waggles his finger. "But do not abandon your daughter or the memory of your mother in the process." He closes his hand. "Painful though the memory may be, bear with it."

Hiding behind the veil, another presence makes itself known. I open my mouth to speak, but my words come out in a hoarse whisper. "And Henry?"

"Could he have used more of your love?" "But it's too late."

"It's never too late to love."

After Father Mike leaves, I make two phone calls. The first call is to Roger. He has been in New York on a business trip, but he got back yesterday. He probably phoned the house and got a busy signal. He might have heard about the fire. It was a front-page story in the *Palo Alto Times*.

He had heard. "Dee, sweetheart, are you okay? I called and called and finally I went by your house and saw what happened. My God! I talked to your neighbors. They said you weren't home when the fire started and that they didn't know where you were. Dee, honey, why didn't you call me?"

He sounded so concerned, and so hurt.

"Roger, I'm so sorry. I am probably still in shock. But I'm calling you now."

"Where are you? Are you okay? Can I come and see you?"

This man really cares. For the first time he isn't offering advice or transportation or help. He is offering me himself, a mooring if I want it.

"Roger, I would love to see you. I've got a place to stay that Laura found for me. Can you come for dinner tonight? I could really use your help thinking through what my options are now."

My next phone call is to Pilar. I give her my new address and phone number and ask about Uncle Iban.

"I'm so glad you called," she says. "I've been trying to reach you. Your uncle had a heart attack. He's been in the hospital, but he's home now. He wants to see you."

Love is patient. Love is kind. Love does not insist on its own way.

"Tell him I'll be there tomorrow."

20

THE MARRIAGE-GO-ROUND

By the time Roger taps on the door, I'm packed and ready to leave in the morning. Minestrone soup is bubbling on the stove and bread is warming in the oven. I've tossed a salad. I love electric appliances—no pilot lights.

"You like my casita?" I set two martinis down on a low table in front of a fire I've had going all day.

"It is charming, Dee. It suits you. How long will you be able to stay here?"

"At least three months. Marianne and Carl are leaving on an extended vacation in Europe. Marianne has asked me to run the co-op for her while she's away. This is pretty perfect, but I know I have some decisions to make. The incident report came back. It was bad wiring."

"You seem to be taking this pretty well."

"I'm sure it will hit me at some point." I lean back into one of the two club chairs that flank the fireplace where cedar and oak logs burn slow and steady. "Honestly, I was pretty stripped to the bone when the house went. I was starting to dig in there, literally—

planting gardens and fixing things to suit myself, doing what I'd been doing for the last several years. I fit myself into the house and the neighborhood, but it wasn't a particularly good fit. It was isolating."

I take a sip from my perfectly chilled martini and nestle my shoulders and neck into the chair's pillow top. "I'm a city girl, for heaven's sake. As it turns out, I'm also an artist." That's the first time I've said that out loud.

I look over at Roger. He approves this assessment with that heart-melting smile of his. Then he shifts forward in his chair, balancing his drink on one knee and drumming his fingers on his other knee. "I have some news too. I've sold my house."

I stand up and raise my glass. "That's something to celebrate. Congratulations."

"Yes." He sips his martini. "So we both have some decisions to make here."

A chill coming in from under the front door stirs up the fire. I continue to stand, warming my backside with the heat coming off the bricks. I want to seal the warmth into my sit bones so I plant myself on the low hearth, play with the olive in my glass, and then blurt it out. "Roger, why have you never married?"

He sets his glass down, leans back in the chair, and crosses his legs. The man is ready to talk.

"I was married. I got married right out of college, but it didn't last."

"What happened?"

"Cecelia wanted a wedding not a marriage. After about six months—after she'd completed her silver, china, and crystal service for twelve—she looked around our little apartment and realized it would be years before she got the dining-room suite to do it all justice."

I'm sipping the last of my martini when he says that. It goes down the wrong way. I sputter and start to cough. He grabs the glass from my hand and hurries to the kitchen to fetch some water for me to drink. When I've regained my composure, he gives me an apologetic smile and continues his story.

"I should have known better. I met her at a sorority party. I knew she liked to party—I guess she thought she'd bring the party home. I was working days at GE and getting my MBA at night, so Cece partied with the guy who was the best man at our wedding."

I was not expecting that kind of candor. I raise a hand to indicate he doesn't need to give me details, but he presses on.

"I don't want to make it sound like this was all her fault. We never should have gotten married. We were both too young. Actually, we're still friends. She married George, the best man, and they have three children. As it turned out, George is away from home way more than I ever was. He's a salesman.

"Cece became an interior decorator. She's really good at it. She helped me get the interior of the Redwood City house in shape for the sale."

That's cozy, I think. *How do you stay friends with an ex who cheated on you? Unless, of course, Roger and George just exchanged roles.*

Roger's not done. "After the divorce, I dated some, but then the war came. I was away in the navy for four years."

Now he gets quiet.

"In 1944 I was attached to a carrier supplying General Clark's Fifth Army in the invasion in Italy. They were fighting the Nazis alongside General Montgomery's British Eighth Army and the newly formed Jewish Brigade. The campaign in Italy was slowing down just as the campaign in France was gearing up for the Normandy invasion. Part of the Brigade's mission was to rescue Jewish children who had been orphaned in the war. I was helping with that. I met a Jewish girl and fell in love. Her name is Dara Burstein."

"And you married her?" Roger is beginning to take on the dimensions of a Lothario.

"We didn't get married, but we did have a child. I have a son, David."

Cue the music. Soap-opera theme songs begin to play in my head. I am a character in one of the stories Leora used to listen to on the radio. I cast myself as the naive and innocent heroine who discovers her lover has a past. I should be alarmed, but instead I'm hooked on the story Roger is telling.

"Where is he?"

"He's in Israel with his mother."

"Do you ever see him?"

"I've been to Israel twice to see him. He's nine years old. Dara and David live on a kibbutz; Dara teaches at the kibbutz school. Her students are the orphans we helped remove from Italy."

"Why didn't you marry her?"

"I wanted to, but she didn't want to come to the United States and I didn't want to spend the rest of my life in Israel. Before I met Dara, I knew nothing about Jewish history. Dara's family escaped a pogrom in Poland and managed to settle in England, where

Dara was born. She didn't consider herself to be English or Polish—she was Jewish. One of the results of the war was that many young Jews discovered their roots in a culture that came from a shared history, not their country of origin."

Then he looks at me. "Cecelia and Dara are as different from each other as they could possibly be, but there is one thing they have in common."

"You?" I wish I had not said that the moment it pops out of my mouth.

Roger laughs. "Yes. They are both strong women who survived me relatively unscathed. No. They are women with much more to them than what I saw on the surface. If I had taken the time to get to know them, I would have realized I had no place in their lives. I guess you could say that I've been through the wars with women."

"And you won't make that mistake again." I start for the kitchen to assemble our dinner.

"I won't get that involved with a woman I don't know very well, if that's what you mean." He follows me over to the stove and ladles soup into the Mexican bowls while I butter the bread.

We eat dinner at a glass-topped table with a wrought- iron base that sits between the kitchenette and the living room. I tell Roger that I'm driving to Bakersfield tomorrow to see Iban and that I'm looking forward to the time the drive will give me to think about my next move. He helps me clear the table and we do the dishes. As I walk him to the door, he has yet another surprise for me. He takes me in his arms and kisses me in a relaxed, familiar way. Then he whispers in my ear. "Let's get to know each other."

❧ Dolores ❧

21

CONFESSIONS

*E*arly the next morning I hit the road. It's a long drive through the Central Valley in a heat thick with crop dust. I stand at my uncle's doorstep, my blouse sticking to my back. I'm massaging my shoulder and lifting my hair off the back of my neck, hoping to catch a breeze off the lake, when a uniformed nurse opens the door before I've even had a chance to knock. She introduces herself as Maria Zabala and ushers me down the hallway to a small bedroom where I drop my suitcase. Over her shoulder, I see Uncle Iban asleep in a hospital bed that's been set up in the living room.

Maria offers me a welcome glass of water and an update on her patient's condition. Iban is in the last stages of cardiopulmonary disease. It's not really the heart attack that caused his rapid decline, she explains. His heart is worn out. Shaking her head and clucking her tongue, she tells me she is leaving for a few hours to check on her family and to go to the store for more food and supplies to stock the refrigerator.

"He will probably wake up in an hour or two." She gives me instructions on what to feed him. "He will be glad to see you."

I don't like being in this room with the curtains drawn. It reminds me of the hours and days I spent sitting idle, watching Leora go. I spot a jigsaw puzzle set up on the dining-room table, something Maria must be working on. I wander over from Iban's bedside to look at it. It's not long before I start popping pieces into a section of blue sky. I scan, test, fit, and push a puzzle piece in place, running my hand over a finished section to feel the seams between the pieces. It soothes me. The puzzle box shows what the finished puzzle will look like. Carmel-by-the-Sea.

When I look up hours later, my uncle is awake, watching me. He smiles. Like the Cheshire cat in Alice in Wonderland, his smile hangs in the air even as the rest of him seems to have gone somewhere else. His smile is not a grin; it's a wistful twist of his dry, cracked lips. I walk over to the bed and ask if I can make him more comfortable. I adjust a pillow under a bony shoulder and help him sit up so he can drink some apple juice. He has lost a shocking amount of weight since the last time I was here.

He asks about what I've been doing since my first trip to see him. I tell him about the fire. He's very concerned that I don't have a place to live. Reaching for my hand, he tells me not to worry. "I won't be around much longer. I'm leaving my house to you, Dolores."

Oh God, no! I don't want two properties to worry about, a burned-out lot in Los Altos and a house in a retirement community in the Tejon Pass. Two places to be responsible for in two different communities where I don't want to live. This is my first inkling that I will likely leave Los Altos, but not for the Central Valley, for heaven's sake.

"People here will take care of you."

What can I say to him? I don't want to be taken care of any more than my mother did. Apparently, these ways of thinking are grooved into us over generations. Who was the first woman in my family who refused to follow a man chasing his dream? How many of my male ancestors left their families to follow a calling to pasture, commerce, or war? And how do I come now to sit at the deathbed of this man I hardly know?

"You know, I saw you and your sister come into this world." Iban stares at the ceiling. "Alaya first, then you. It was the happiest day of Alonso's life. He loved you both so much."

"He must have been very upset when she died." I'm trying to keep him talking. Tears spring into the eyes of this man who has very little time left.

"I have to tell you, Dolores." The tears stop. "I have to break a promise I made to your mother and father."

He is struggling for breath now.

"This is very hard." He looks at me with eyes that plead for forgiveness.

"They are both gone, Iban. What is it you need to tell me?"

I can barely hear his next words. "Alaya didn't die. Alonso took her back to Spain with him."

"My mother kept me and my father took my sister?"

"Yes."

"Why?"

"Leora couldn't start the new life she wanted with two little girls." Iban seems to draw renewed energy from somewhere. His voice gets stronger. His limp hands resurrect themselves in gestures that tell the story. "I offered to help, but she didn't want to stay here. The two of them came up with this plan. It was a way they could guarantee that you both would have a good life."

"So Alaya didn't die here, she died in Spain."

"She didn't die, Dolores. She's not dead."

"She's alive? In Spain?"

"Yes."

"How do you know?"

"Pilar keeps track of her. Alaya keeps track of us. All of us." He looks at me and I can see the crafty young man he once was. I'm not feeling much sympathy now.

"I have a twin sister who has always known about me, but who has never tried to contact me?" He closes his eyes. "Everyone knows this but me?"

Iban has finished telling his story. He never opens his eyes again.

I check into a motel in Bakersfield and stay for a week between Iban's death and the memorial service. In his will I discover that he's left me not one but two houses. It seems he held on to the little place he lived in on East Truxtun Avenue before he moved outside of town. This is more than an embarrassment of riches, it is a nightmare. Just when I am trying to free myself, property is piling up. But I have no time to think about that. Iban also indicated in his will that he wished to be memorialized at church and buried in Union Cemetery.

My only experience with this sort of thing was Henry's brief graveside military service arranged by a chaplain and my mother's impromptu interment that didn't require much planning. I am unprepared for the production of laying Uncle Iban to rest.

Crowds of people attend the viewing at the mortuary in the evening. The next morning a line of cars forms a parade to Saint Francis of Assisi. Uncle Iban attends the service in an elaborate flower-draped coffin. Also in attendance are eight dark-suited pallbearers, all looking as if they might join him in his supine state at any moment. They are his cronies from the oil company. The church is packed to overflowing.

The pallbearers escort Uncle Iban out of the church after the service and back to his carriage, where it processes on to the cemetery. The graveside service attracts less attention but more oratory. What Uncle Iban lacked in actual family he made up for in friends, neighbors, and countrymen. Stories of his humor, his generosity, his contributions to the community, his ability to spin a yarn, and his love for animals and small children accompany each spade of dirt sprinkled ceremoniously on his coffin. The man was a saint if you can believe these people.

Next stop is the Basque Club, where bandy-legged tables cower under huge plates piled high with food. Basque musicians pull instruments from their cases and begin tuning up on a stage. Costumed dancers arrive. There are more people here than at the church and cemetery combined.

Pilar appears at my side.

"Your uncle was much loved in this community."

"I see that."

"I wish you had known him when he was younger." "I was not given that opportunity."

A cloud of indecision passes across Pilar's pretty face. She takes my hand and pulls me away from the noisy crowd to a seat toward the back of the room.

"I'm sorry that so many secrets were kept from you. It's not my job to interfere in the decisions the families make. I stepped out of bounds when I made an inquiry about Leora. May I ask, did you get the answers you were looking for from Iban before he died?"

"Do you mean did he tell me that my twin sister is still alive? Yes, he did. Did he explain why this is a secret that everyone knows except me? No, he didn't. Can you explain that to me?"

Pilar's face shows no reaction to the bitterness in my voice. "I can put you in touch with Alaya if you like."

"I don't like any of this. I've been lied to all my life for no reason I can discover." I stand up and look down at her. "Alaya knows who I am and where I am. If she wants to get in touch with me, she has always had the ability to do so."

Pilar appears deflated and sad. A twinge of guilt stabs at my heart.

"Look, I know this isn't your fault. It's a heck of a job you've inherited here, babysitting these people." I turn to leave, then I turn back to her. "You can have the houses and everything in them. Just send me whatever papers I need to sign."

I'm going home. But I'll have to figure out where that is.

❧ *Dolores* ☙

22

GIFTS

I slam the car door shut and stride through the doors of Saint Matthew's into Father Mike's office. After I spill my anger, he sympathizes with a click of his tongue that erupts into a soft chuckle. "And you left your uncle's property to the Basque community out of love and compassion, is that right, Dee?"

"No. If I could have thrown it at Pilar, I would have." My anger has softened now. "That's awful, isn't it?"

We move on to discuss my favorite topic, Leora. "Father Mike, I spent months going through my mother's stuff. I couldn't give it away fast enough. And the few things I wanted burned up in the fire. Most people are devastated when they lose everything. Me? I felt free."

"No regrets?"

"I am sorry I lost most of the photos. Placing them in collages was like meditating. I was beginning to get some insights into my mother."

"Such as?"

"She had an inquiring mind. She was very observant. Her relationships didn't go deep, but she knew and appreciated many different kinds of people. The courtroom really was her place. If she'd been a man, she'd have made a good attorney or judge. She had that 'old boy' way about her."

Father Mike stands up and moves around the desk to where I am sitting. He lays a hand on my shoulder. "How does that fit your picture of a mother who divided her children and sent one away?"

I look up at him, surprising myself with a ready answer. "It helps me understand why she did it. She thought it was the right thing to do."

"Let's take a walk." I follow Father Mike out through the orchard. We enter the chapel and stand in front of the columbarium. His eyes turn to the urn that contains Leora's ashes and the two empty urns on either side.

"Who do you suppose . . . "

I get his train of thought. "Alaya and I," I whisper.

"Your mother was not religious, but she did come to understand that what happens in this world is not all there is. She knew it was unlikely that Alaya would ever return, but she wanted to make room for the possibility. She never forgot that she had two daughters."

We continue our walk through the orchard. "Dee, when Valerie gets home, tell her right away about the fire. Let her be part of the decision about what you do with the property."

"You think I was hasty in giving away my uncle's houses?"

"You didn't give them away, you threw them away. There's a difference."

Back at the casita, I give Laura a call and invite her to dinner. She hesitates and then says that it's Fred's poker night. But she decides that she can get them started with drinks and snacks and then sneak out for a bite if I don't mind eating late.

Why does she feel she has to sneak around? This Fred does not impress me. How will I bring this up in our conversation? Because that's what I intend to do. I can't continue to ignore my suspicion that something isn't right in the McMillan household.

My next call is to Roger at work. We arrange to meet after work so I can tell him about my trip. I have never had so many people to account to in my life—Father Mike, Roger, Laura, Marianne, and now it seems I will have to cast Valerie as an adult and include her in my circle.

Peter has been to see me—for the last time, probably. He told me that Valerie is recuperating well and plans to be home for the holidays. He'll be going home to Ohio to see his parents. The way he talked, I think his relationship with Valerie has changed. I don't ask questions though. I did extract a promise from him that he won't mention the fire in any letters to her. There's nothing she can do, so why trouble her.

I have the afternoon shift at the co-op office. As I walk down Main Street, shop windows compete for my attention. In the dress shop, headless mannequins party in holiday dresses, silver trays of crystal glasses at their feet. In the gift shop window, coffee-table books inspire lust for food and travel. Hanging on a wall visible from the street, an impressionist landscape and a watercolor amaryllis invite purchase at the co-op. One of my collages is also on display.

When I get to the office, I open the cash box. Among the pile of checks are several made out to me for sales of my work. I will have to build up more inventory. Nervous energy lights a fire of appreciation in my heart. It's not so much about the money—it's about the testimony. I have a public, people who are willing to see the world in new ways, people who care about the things I care about.

Dusk comes early now. Reflections of Christmas lights shining in store windows shimmer in black puddles on the street. I don't bother to shield myself with an umbrella against the soft rain that dusts my head and shoulders as I puddle-hop across to meet Roger at Mac's Tea Room. We sit in the far corner of the cozy neighborhood watering hole, privileged first customers early in an evening after the afternoon tipplers have cleared out to make room for those who are still finishing the day's work. Putting our heads together over Manhattans, I give Roger a brief rundown of my trip to Bakersfield. Then I tell him I'm meeting Laura for dinner and why I'm concerned about her.

"You think her husband knocks her around? Have you ever seen bruises?"

"Well, no, I haven't, but she seems to be afraid of him, or at least very careful about upsetting him. That's a clue, isn't it?" I sip my drink slowly. I don't intend to have a cloudy head when I meet Laura.

"Be careful about assuming, Dee. There could be another explanation."

"You think I shouldn't pry?"

"I don't think that at all. I think you should give her a chance to talk if she wants to."

Good idea. I have such wise people in my life.

Our conversation drifts. Roger invites me to the company Christmas party.

"Oh, I don't think so."

"C'mon, Dee, let's show them how great you're doing, how great we're doing."

My thoughts go back to the cocktail dresses I admired earlier—the little black one. No, the red one; definitely the red one. Pilar looks sexy in red and our coloring is so similar. It's strange how often she pops into my head.

"Okay. Let's do it. Let's wow them."

Roger heads out to look at apartments. Now that his house has sold, he's decided to move closer to work and to me, and rent for a while, at least until he gets his money out of escrow. I walk down the street to meet Laura.

She's waiting in her car in front of Belluci's. Hopping out as soon as she sees me, she gives me a hug and we go in and grab a table.

"I love their lasagna," she says, and then peppers me with questions about my trip. We each order a glass of Gemello's Cabernet and Laura natters on about gossip she's heard at our little artists' colony. I don't know how I'm going to raise the subject of Fred, so I just do it.

"Laura, tell me about your husband. Where did you meet?"

Her face colors a bit. "Oh, we met in college."

"Well, tell me about him. Will I ever meet him?"

Laura stares into her glass and then slowly raises it to her tightly pressed lips. She barely relaxes enough to sip a little wine. I can't tell if she is buying time, trying to figure out how to change the subject, or bracing herself before she finally comes clean with the truth.

"I guess we know each other well enough that I can tell you this." She is clearly uncomfortable. "Fred was a big, handsome football player when I met him. He was funny and smart and popular. He still is all those things. We got married right after college, and Fred went to work in his father's car dealership, but he wasn't happy. He wanted to be a mechanical engineer. He has a very logical mind. The war came along and he went into the Army. They tested him and discovered how smart he is, and they put him in charge of some sort of artificial intelligence project. He really liked the work.

"To make a long story short, he was playing football with his men during recreation one afternoon, and he got tackled too hard and got knocked out. The blow to his head aggravated an old injury. He had convulsions and things just went downhill from there. The Army gave him a medical discharge and that was a one-two punch. The injury and the depression triggered some sort of . . . illness."

Laura stops talking and looks down at her plate. When she looks up, she has tears in her eyes. "You're the first person I've ever told this to. I don't like to make people uncomfortable."

I reach across the table for her hand and squeeze it. "Laura, you can tell me anything. God knows, I've told you enough about my crazy life. The way you talk about Fred, I was afraid he was hitting you. He doesn't hit you, does he?"

Laura looks horrified. "Oh no! Never! Is that what you thought?"

I lower my head, my thoughts swirling. "One thing I'm confused about—you said Fred has a good job at IBM?"

"Oh, he's very smart. He's a good worker. It's just that he has to have a certain kind of environment or he gets anxious. He's fine as long as he keeps to a routine. We have a small set of friends we've known for a long time that he's okay with. IBM assigned him a partner who runs interference so Fred can stay focused on his work. They've been real good to us. It's just that new situations upset him and new people make him nervous."

"And that's why no children?"

"That's why. Fred wanted to try for a family, but his doctor advised against that. Fred still has hopes though." She laughs. "He's not very realistic about how unnerving kids can be." She laughs again.

We order cannoli for dessert and have some coffee. "I'm glad I told you, Dee. It's terrible that I made Fred sound like a wife beater!"

"We all make lots of assumptions based on very little information, don't we?"

And then the conversation turns to holiday plans and the trio of cocktail dresses in the window across the street.

On the day of the GE Christmas party, I roll up the sheerest nylon stockings I have ever worn and hook them to a new girdle. Then I slither into the silky red sheath dress with a boat neck that forms a deep V in back.

Roger has told me to wear only earrings.

"Won't that be chilly?" I answered, and he laughed.

He shows up at the door all tuxed out, with a brightly wrapped present he puts under my tiny Christmas tree and a small velvet box he places in my hand. Inside I find an oval 14K diamond-and-garnet drop-pendant necklace. It looks beautiful with my dress.

"I like buying jewelry for my girl. Next year we'll get you the earrings."

"You'll have to wait for your gift," I tell him, as we head out the door. "I'm very traditional; Christmas Eve for you."

We've planned a quiet celebration at the casita, just dinner at home and the midnight service at Saint Matthew's. Valerie is flying home on Christmas Day and I've set aside that day for her. The Watsons are due home on New Year's Day and I'm determined to have a plan by then. I'm in danger of overstaying my welcome. I have some ideas I want to run by Valerie that I haven't told anyone else.

Roger and I drive through heavy traffic to San Francisco. GE is having their party in a ballroom at the Fairmont Hotel. San Francisco is an elegant lady during the holidays, wrapped in furs and dripping in diamonds; if her slip is a bit tawdry dockside, all the more fun.

The party is in full throttle—I'm learning aviation terms now. Roger seats us with his coworkers and their wives. Elaine spots us right away and strides across the room to give me a chilly nod and lay a hand on Roger's arm.

"We've got a seat for you at Mr. Bradley's table."

"Oh, that's not necessary, Elaine. I'd really rather sit with my people." He gives her his warmest smile. She shrugs and walks off.

"That's not a career-limiting move?" I ask.

"More for him than for me." He ushers me to the dance floor. "Dick Bradley doesn't get that these tech companies are going to need to be managed less as fiefdoms, where management and employees don't mix, and more as environments where everyone works together. That's why after the first of the year I'm going to work for Ralph Cordiner."

"The president of GE?"

"Yes. He's asked me to join his staff and help re-shape management."

"That's wonderful, Roger."

He pulls me to him and we foxtrot around the dance floor. Heading back to our table I ask him, "Does this mean you might be moving east?"

It's hard to talk above the din of music, conversation, and clinking tableware. He bends down to catch my question. "That's not clear yet. You and I have some talking to do."

The rest of the evening, we make pleasant conversation with the people at our table, eat a nice filet mignon, and enjoy the dance floor.

On the drive home, there is no more talk of future plans, his or mine. I'm dozy. In companionable silence, we listen to Christmas music on the radio, Bing Crosby and Dean Martin. As we pass through the gates to the Watson estate, the lights are on in the main house and a is car parked in the circular driveway. Apparently, the Watsons have returned home early.

Over the next few days, Roger and I are content to let the old year run out without worrying about what the new one will hold for us. On Christmas Eve, I unwrap a heavy box and find several new lenses for my camera. He is equally delighted with the leather flight bag I have given him to replace his old one. Then we stuff ourselves with ham, green beans, twice-baked potatoes, and cheesecake, and somehow manage to brave the chilly air to attend midnight Christmas Eve service.

❧ Dolores ❧

23

HOMECOMING

I drive to the San Francisco airport on Christmas Day to meet Valerie's plane. When she spots me, she catapults through the gate like a contestant in a potato-sack race. Her left leg is encased in a cast that starts below her knee and ends just short of where her nicely pedicured toes stick out. What looks like a rubber bathtub stopper is glued to the heel of the cast. She pogos up to me, balancing her weight on her heel, and throws a free arm around my neck. I grab the bag she is carrying, and off we go to get her luggage. Soon we're on the freeway, which is eerily free of vehicles on Christmas morning.

Valerie chats nonstop without giving me any information whatsoever. She talks about her little studio apartment in Barcelona, how welcome her editor and his family made her feel, how good it was to see Peter. She describes being mugged, in detail, and thanks me for helping her get another driver's license and passport. All this chatter seems designed to prevent me from asking her what is going on with Peter or what she plans to do with the rest of her life. We are getting closer to Los Altos, and I have to find a way to break Valerie's monologue and tell her we aren't going to the house on Lundy Lane.

Distracted by a passing Ferrari with a blonde at the wheel and sporty-looking gent in the passenger seat, Valerie whoops, "Oh, somebody must have been a very good girl!"

I agree and then grab the reins of this conversation. "Val, I have something to tell you. I wouldn't say it's bad news really, but it's news that might shock you."

"Let me guess! You and Roger are getting married." "No! Why would that be bad news?"

"You said it wasn't bad news."

"Would you be shocked if Roger and I got married?" This is a ridiculous conversation. Roger and I aren't even talking about getting married.

"So what's the news?"

"Your grandmother's house burned down."

"What? No! When? How? Why didn't you tell me?"

"Slow down, Valerie, I'm telling you now. I didn't want to write this news in a letter. I wanted to tell you in person."

"Did Peter know about this? He didn't say a thing." "He didn't know when he left for Spain. I drove home one evening from Saint Matthew's and the house was on fire. It pretty much burned to the ground. The fire was caused by a short in some faulty wiring in the kitchen."

"Oh, Mom, that's horrible. Everything in the house burned? You didn't get anything out?"

"Laura got there before I did. She got some of my collages and my camera out while it was still safe. The house went up pretty quickly. There wasn't anything they could do to save it."

Valerie burst into tears. "I loved that house."

"I know you did, honey."

"So," she sniffed, "where are you living now?"

"For right now, I'm living in a guesthouse on the Watson estate." She looks at me, puzzled and suspicious.

"Marianne Watson owns the art co-op where I'm working now. That's a long story for another time. You and I are going to need to talk about where we're going to live, but not today. You've had a long flight. Let's get you back to the casita and let you rest."

"The casita? You sound pretty dug in."

I pull through the gates and around to my cozy temporary home. Valerie whistles. "Nice digs! You really know how to fall on your feet, Mom."

I give Valerie my bedroom. I've made up a bed for myself on the couch. She objects, but not very hard. We eat leftover ham and cheesecake, and I put my Christmas gift in her lap. It's the collage of Leora. An oak tree forms her spine and branches out. Eyes look down from the leaves on the tree. More eyes twinkle among the leaves piled on the ground. A fiery opal plucked from one of Valerie's favorite pieces of Leora's jewelry shines among the dying leaves.

"I hope you don't mind that I took her brooch apart." "Oh no, it's so meaningful, what you've done here. Is this the only collage that's left?"

"Maybe not. You'll just have to wait and see." I have another one tucked away for her birthday. It's of a woman in her prime with a young girl by her side, their laughing faces reflected in a mirror as they primp. Snippets of modern and vintage apparel from catalogs provide context for the photos. Bits of ribbon, feathers, and veiling give it texture.

"Valerie, I'm sorry we don't have anything left of your grandmother's things, but that's all they were— things. What's important is the legacy she left us. She was a strong, talented, smart woman. So are you. So am I. We got that from her. The things we leave behind aren't important. What's important are the memories we carry forward and what we do because of them."

"Wow, Mom, I've never heard you be so philosophical."

Then she gives me my gift. It's not wrapped. She places a book on my lap. "I know you won't be able to read this. It's in Spanish. But an English language version will be released in the United States sometime this year. This is my promise that I'll get you an advance copy."

I hold up the book. "Is this your thesis?"

"No. It's my first novel. I had anticipated publishing it only in Spanish, but the publisher has bigger plans, so . . . "

"You write novels? I thought you were studying Spanish literature and publishing your thesis. Why didn't you tell me?"

I hate that phrase—*Why didn't you tell me?* I've tried to remove it from my lexicon, but it keeps sneaking back in. My emotions are fragile and teary again—but not angry.

"Oh well, you know, novelists are like that. They keep it all a secret until it's a success. I honestly didn't think it would go anywhere."

The book's glossy cover shocks me. The art on the cover is more than vaguely reminiscent of the postcard my father sent to my mother. Valerie fidgets and sets her eyes firmly on the fruit bowl on the table.

"Mom," she says to the fruit bowl in her teacher voice, "first I want to remind you that novelists write fiction. It's inevitable that they put some of themselves and their own stories in their work, but that gets tangled up with the story they really want to tell."

"I don't understand." I turn to her for an explanation, but she continues to look away.

"I don't want to tell you about the story I wrote. I want you to read it and then I want us to talk about it." She looks into my face. "Okay?"

I'm treading on thin ice here. Valerie is entrusting me with her secret. She is trusting me not to make her regret this gift. *Love—it does not insist on its own way; it's not irritable or resentful.* Funny, these words don't come from my head. God's word bubbles up from my heart. I don't have to have answers to all my questions right now. The answers will come.

I place the book aside. "Okay. I have something else to tell you. Your uncle Iban died while you were gone. I'm sorry you never had a chance to meet him, but he left us some property."

RESOLUTIONS

Mom and I are back at Clarke's for a noontime burger on New Year's Eve Day. She wants to talk to me about her plans, but I have a plan of my own. Today I'm going to declare my independence. I wait for her to bite into her burger and then I lay it on her.

"Mom, I'm going to get my PhD." Her eyes get big and she starts chewing really fast. I rev up the volume before she can swallow. "I plan to teach at a university, Stanford, I hope. I'm moving out of student housing—it's expensive and it's for students. I'm a scholar not a student. I'll be hanging out in the library most of the time so I just need a place to shower and change clothes."

Mom holds up a finger while she swallows hard. I reach for her hand that she is flapping in the air and lower it to the table.

"Mom, I'm going off your payroll. I will pay for my PhD myself." I tell her about my advance from my Spanish publisher. She's nodding and smiling, about to drink from a glass of iced tea when I tell her the crazy part. "I want to buy the lot on Lundy Lane from you."

Her glass of tea slips out of her hand and lands with a thud on the table, splashing tea everywhere. I grab a napkin and mop up the spill.

"Why?"

"It will be my stake in the ground."

"That's all that's left, you know, just the ground."

"Mom, this valley is going to grow! In ten years, you won't recognize it. That is going to be some very valuable property someday."

"You want it for an investment? What are you going to do with it? Let it sit there and then sell it? The neighbors won't like that."

"I plan to build a house on the lot, but not for awhile."

"What do you have in mind?"

"I want to own land. I want to build myself a house. If I work hard and save my money, I'll be able to build just what I want in a few years. My work will have me traveling a lot, but I want a place to come back to that's home. It will even have a name. People will know it as the Moraga place."

My mother's lips press into a familiar straight line when I pronounce Lita's last name. Then she surprises me.

"I like the idea, Valerie. We'll go to the county and transfer the deed into your name."

I protest, but she cuts me off.

"I do have some say in how this all goes."

"Deal!" We shake hands.

People are knocking off early and crowding into Clarke's. We should give up our table, but now that I've hooked Mom on my idea, I want to reel her in. "The house will have a writer's studio for me and an artist's studio for you, small bedrooms and big work-rooms to fit our lives."

I stop when I see that famous Moraga brow etch a V between her widely spaced brown eyes as she frowns.

"You assume a lot when you think I plan to live with you, missy! You don't plan to get married ever?"

"Well, I've given that a lot of thought. I'm heading into my late twenties and it hasn't happened yet. There was a time when I thought Peter and I might get married, but he's chasing a career in baseball and we both know I'm not a fan. There was a man in Barcelona . . . "

Mom sits very still. I choose my words carefully. "He may be coming over to study at Stanford, but I'm not holding my breath. I think marriage isn't something you plan for, it's something you leave the door open for—I'm leaving the door open."

That seems to satisfy her.

I pay the bill, but we have more to talk about. Mom's got it made in the shade at the casita, but this sweet deal is coming to an end. I suggest we go for drive in the hills before we head home.

My ankle is starting to throb. I adjust the seat back as far as it will go, prop my leg on the dashboard, and wait for Mom to say something.

"Iban left us his house at Pine Mountain Club and some little house in Bakersfield near the railroad tracks. You have no interest in either property, do you?"

We're driving out toward the Duveneck ranch. "Probably not, but I'd like to see them."

"I have an idea. Do you have time to make a trip to Bakersfield?"

"With you?"

"No, I was thinking you might like to go by yourself. There is a young woman you should meet who is about your age. She's the executor of Iban's estate. You and Pilar, that's her name, have a lot in common. She's a scholar too."

"What does she study?"

"Basque culture and history."

Mom's tone is neutral when she says this, her expression blank. She's trying too hard, but the idea is irresistible.

"After I get this cast off, I could drive over to Bakersfield and represent you—figure out how to handle the sale. I'd need to borrow your car though. You sure you don't want to go with me?" I'm testing her.

"I'm sure."

We head back to the casita because Mom has a date with Roger. I'm frosted that this is the first New Year's Eve that I don't have date, but I guess I better get used to it. When we walk into the casita, Mom heads straight for her bedroom and returns jangling her car keys, which she places in my hand along with the pink slip to her old Chevy sedan. Then she grabs my other hand and leads me out back to show me her brand-new 1955 Chevy Bel Air.

"That is unreal, Mom! Did Roger buy you that?"

"Of course not. I bought me that." Again, her eyebrows squiggle over her eyes and she lifts one corner of her lip in a comical grimace. "I may have to live in it."

I'm still waiting for her to tell me her plans. I guess I should have asked.

"Mom, I'm sorry I haven't asked you what you are planning to do. All we seem to have talked about is me."

"That's okay." She seems sincere. "I'm still working on my plan. I'd like to settle things with Roger tonight before I tell you what I have in mind."

That doesn't sound like a very promising evening for Roger. My earlier fit of pique dissipates. After what I've been through with men, the prospect of a warm bed and a good book looks like the better bargain. I wouldn't want to be on either end of what I imagine will be the giving and receiving of bad news.

❧ Dolores ❧

25

COURAGE

Roger and I spend a quiet New Year's Eve together. For two single people, we stay home more than I ever expected we would, which is strange since neither of us has a home. We've found homey places to call our own though. One is the Babbling Brook restaurant in Santa Cruz. We toast 1955 at a small table tucked in a corner loft of the rustic lodge. The creek water below us glimmers on smooth rocks.

Roger tells me he is expected on the East Coast within a month for a six-month stint under the tutelage of Ralph Cordiner. After that, he'll be coming back to the plant in Palo Alto.

"Ralph is pioneering a new decentralized management system." Roger places his elbows on the table and tells me more than I want to know. The gist of it is that he will help design the financial part of the new system and then move back to the Bay Area and be a guinea pig. But that's not all he is trying to design. He barely conceals his excitement as he tries to express his concern over how we will manage a long-distance relationship.

"Dee, how about you take over the lease on my apartment while I'm gone? That will give you six more months to decide what you want to do."

He seems very pleased with himself for figuring all this out—such the manager he is. He assures me that regular trips back to the Bay Area are in his contract and that we will continue to see each other. He's about to steer the conversation in the direction of defining our relationship with a pledge of exclusivity, but I'm not sure whether he intends for this to reassure me or him.

"How about I don't take a lease on your apartment. I have some plans of my own, and they don't include an apartment in Palo Alto, unless I could rent your second bedroom to store my stuff."

The assumptions Roger is making amuse me. The man who assumed his first wife would be happy in a cramped apartment while he was growing his career; the man who assumed his wartime lover would follow him back to the United States with their son; the man who swore he would never again make assumptions about what a woman wanted is still a man after all. The assumption that a woman will make a man the absolute center of her life dies hard.

He begins to apologize, but I stop him.

"I should have told you what I'm planning, but there just hasn't been time." He is at the wheel of my new Bel Air, which I insisted we test drive in the mountains this evening and he agreed, but only if he could drive. He drives slowly on the curvy mountain road we have all to ourselves at one in the morning. The headlights chase the leaves that blow across the road. A storm is brewing.

"Marianne and I have been talking. She thought I did a great job of managing the co-op while she and Dick were in Europe. She wants to open another co-op in Carmel, and she wants me to run it for her."

"Dee, that is an amazing opportunity." This man gets more points for what he doesn't say than what he does say. He doesn't say, "But what about us?"

When I announce my plan to Valerie, her first words are "But, Mom, what about Roger?"

"What about him? He's going to Connecticut. I'm going to Carmel."

"Yes, but he's coming back to live in Palo Alto in six months. You'll be in Carmel. How's that going to work?"

This comes from the girl who ditched Peter because she didn't want to be a camp follower? I say this out loud.

"It's not the same thing,"

"How's that?"

"Well, I couldn't travel all over the country and do my work."

"Who says you would have to travel? Lots of baseball wives stay home while their husbands are on the road."

"Yeah, you did that, and it wasn't such a great marriage." She claps her hand over her mouth. "I'm sorry I said that, Mom."

"No, you're right. Your father and I made the best of a bad situation. Two wars, assignments to posts I thought were too remote. We made it work, like lots of Army couples do, but it wasn't ideal. The Army comes first for a career officer. I didn't realize when we got married that it would be Henry's career."

The truth is, I wanted Valerie to have a stable home. I hated being dragged from hotel room to hotel room by a mother who didn't concern herself with my future. I wanted Valerie to have a good education, not be uprooted in the middle of a school year every time Henry got new orders. These thoughts are a revelation to me, but what comes out of my mouth next is even more startling.

"Valerie, I didn't know what I wanted out of life. I ended up in jobs that didn't suit me. But it's working out. The bank and GE were my boot camp. I picked up skills that will help me manage an art co-op—business skills that other artists don't have but need to be successful. I can work in an environment that I love, I can do my art, and I can live in one of the most beautiful places on earth."

"So you're giving up Roger?" my emancipated daughter asks me in a small voice. "I like him."

"I'm not giving him up. Like you, I'm leaving the door open." I give her a wink.

Roger and I did not have the "where is this relationship going" conversation before he left for the East Coast. I moved my boxes into his spare bedroom and he sublet his apartment to a coworker who was getting divorced. Our agreement is that we will share the details of our new lives in letters and a once-a-week phone call.

On Saint Valentine's Day, I give a fond last look at the casita in my rearview mirror as I drive away. My first stop is Lundy Lane. Driving slowly past the vacant lot, I'm surprised to see that Valerie hasn't wasted any time. In the two months since she's been in possession of the Moraga place, she's had the lot cleared of brush and debris. If a small tract of land could have a facial expression, this one would be beaming with hope.

I park the car down at the end of the lane in front of Laura's house and walk up her driveway. Fred will be at work so this is a risk I can take. Laura spots me from the kitchen window and throws open the front door. She smiles even more broadly when she sees the parting gift I have in my hands for her. We sit on her front-porch swing and she unwraps the collage I have made for her. It's the first one I've done that isn't about Leora.

"Oh my gosh, Dee!" Music notes cut from an old songbook form leaves in an orchard of trees. Somehow the piece sings with the movement of an afternoon breeze. Laura moves a finger over the signature: Dee Moraga. *My nom d'artiste.* "I own a Dee Moraga!"

She laughs and we hug. Laura promises she will come and visit me in Carmel, but how can she disrupt Frank's routine like that?

My last stop is St. Matthew's.

"How will that work?" Father Mike asks me when I describe the new path Roger and I are walking.

"I'm not sure. It does sound like a Hollywood movie, doesn't it?" I look for a way to change the subject. I don't have to look very far. "Father Mike, I want to thank you for advising me to get Valerie involved in the Bakersfield deal. I have a feeling some good will come of that."

Father Mike is looking thoughtfully out the window over my shoulder. He spots my new car parked in view of his office, packed with boxes of my art supplies and a couple of suitcases. He returns his gaze to my face. "Dee, I wish you could see yourself."

"I see myself every day in the mirror." I'm having to get a little too artful with the Revlon pencils and pots. I don't like spending time on my face that I could be spending on my collages.

He raps his knuckles on his desk. "We're both getting older, but the little lines I see in your face—and, my dear, they are little—are from work and wisdom, not worry and resentment. You've done well, working all this out."

"It's not completely worked out."

"True— you don't know whether this new arrangement with Roger will keep the spark going. You don't know whether Alaya—joy—will ever return."

That's a new thought. I always assumed that if there was to be a reunion, it would have to be initiated by me.

"Dee, keep asking the big questions. Keep seeking truth in your art and your life. Keep knocking on the door." Father Mike is nodding his head. He can't resist a sermon. He picks up his Bible and holds it in front of me. "This business of knocking—it's in Matthew and in Revelation. Dee, I believe that the doors to our hearts can malfunction. Our Lord opens doors to understanding, but only if we keep the hinges properly maintained. You might say that our faith hinges on knowing what we hope for and believing it's there for us."

He chuckles over his pun, then sets his Bible back down and beats on his chest with vigor. "Prime that pump you have in there with love for God and compassion for others, and for yourself. God will help you do that; understanding will come."

"'Now faith is the substance of things hoped for, the evidence of things not seen.' Hebrews eleven, verse one," I say, nodding my head.

His eyes widen and his face breaks into a smile. "You've been reading your Bible!"

He gets up and comes around his desk to envelop me in a big Father Mike hug. Our chests and bellies bump in a way that affirms deep friendship, and my eyes sting with tears.

"You give me courage, Father Mike."

"We all need a lot of that in life, don't we?"

❧ *Valerie* ❦

26

OSPATU

Driving through the Central Valley is like living in a Salvador Dali painting—endlessly odd. This road goes on forever. Ridges of brown dirt whizz by me and I'm in danger of falling asleep. I have to slap myself several times. Not a good idea to count the sheep I see grazing alongside the highway. Mom's old Chevy is holding up pretty well though.

I tune the radio looking for a Spanish station to see if I can find local news; it's not the Spanish I learned, but I can make it out. Flipping the radio dial for more interesting listening, I come across a fuzzy station broadcasting something regional. I've been doing a lot of study lately on the Basques. I'm pretty sure this broadcast is in Euskara, the Basque language that went underground when Franco came to power. Of course, I don't understand a word of it. I tune to a pop station and crank up some Smiley Lewis. I'm awake now.

I park on the street by the Wool Growers Café. Pilar has suggested that we meet there for an early dinner. A lovely girl who looks like a Spanish version of Audrey Hepburn walks out the front door and meets me on the sidewalk. She thrusts out her hand in greeting and shakes mine warmly.

"Are you hungry? I should think so after that long drive, unless you stopped somewhere for a burger. I hope not, because I have a treat for you."

"I stopped for gas. My body was too numb from the drive to do anything but keep going so I just grabbed some peanuts and a Coke to keep myself awake."

"Oh, I know. I drive up to Berkeley about once a month. I'm working on a PhD in social and cultural anthropology."

Pilar puts an arm around my shoulder and guides me into the restaurant. My eyes adjust to the dark interior. A well-stocked bar runs the length of the restaurant on one side and homey tables and booths cozy up to one another on the other side. The walls are crowded with photographs of families, civic groups, and homesteads. The head of a ram eyes me from over the cash register that sits on the bar. It's that awkward time of day when staff is just beginning to arrive to serve the evening meal.

I turn my attention back to Pilar. "I'm starting work on a PhD in Spanish literature. What's your field of interest?"

"How Basque culture gets transmitted in the diaspora in the U.S. It's a huge topic. There are Basque communities thriving in many states, California, Idaho, and Nevada to name a few. It's a daunting task."

"I'll bet. My dissertation is on the influence of the Spanish Civil War on Spanish literature."

"An equally absorbing project." As we head for the booth that Pilar points out, we are greeted by a young woman about our age. "Valerie, I'd like you to meet my friend Mayie. She and her husband opened this restaurant just last year."

Mayie smiles broadly and clicks her tongue. "You are in such luck! Roasted lamb is on the menu today."

Pilar gives her friend a playful shove. "Roasted lamb is on your menu every day!"

It's not long before plates of food begin appearing, and Pilar and I dig into the best meal I've ever eaten. Mayie plunks dish after dish down in front of us. A bowl of beans and a bowl of sauce appear with a tureen of vegetable soup. Pilar instructs me to ladle the beans and salsa into my soup. The bartender, Mayie's husband, sets an unlabeled bottle of red wine down on our table. Then pickled calves tongue, beets, cottage cheese, blue cheese, lettuce, roast lamb, bread, baby onions, and corn parade across the table. A honey taste lingers on my tongue; the fragrance of the meal oozes from my pores.

"We Basques are very enterprising," Pilar tells me. "In a few years, we won't be herding sheep, we'll own the herds. We'll be serving lamb in the restaurants we own and selling our wool to manufacturers. We'll travel back to Euskal Herria to connect with our families. The big question is, will succeeding generations value that connection . . . "

"Or will they secede emotionally and not care; I know . . . "

"Precisely. We have a motto, *Ospatu, Hezitu, Betikotu.* Celebrate, Educate, Perpetuate."

People are starting to fill up the tables around us. Once again, the restaurant door squeaks open and bangs shut. Before I have a chance to look over, a young man has slid into the booth next to Pilar. He reaches over to an empty table next to ours and grabs a clean fork. Then he stabs a piece of lamb off Pilar's plate and stuffs it into his mouth.

"Yum!" he says, winking at me.

"Ander!" Pilar appears more glad to see this young man than offended by the theft. "Valerie, this is my little brother, Ander, and I apologize for his rudeness."

He reaches across the table to shake my hand. "Andy," he corrects his sister, "and I am very pleased to meet you."

Andy isn't so little. He's well over six feet tall and gorgeous. If this is what Lita experienced when she happened into town, it's no wonder she didn't get out without my mother in tow. Something churns inside of me. I turn red, pull my hand out from underneath the table, and offer it to him.

"What are you two yakking about?"

"Important stuff," Pilar says. "You can stay and listen or . . . "

"No, I have to get out to the ranch to see about the horses." He smiles at me. "Will I see you later?"

"I'm going to take Valerie over to Noriega's after dinner," Pilar says.

"I'll drive back in to town and meet you there later, then." He pulls his long legs out from under the table and lopes off. He wears the Bakersfield uniform, a plaid Western shirt belted into a tight pair of jeans adorned with a huge silver buckle, worn cowboy boots, and a black cowboy hat.

"Don't let that getup fool you. My brother is a newly minted attorney. Despite the hat, he's one of the good guys. He represents our interests at the Farm Labor Bureau."

Mayie brings us coffee and a custard-filled cake. Then the conversation shifts. "I have an offer on your house in town that I want to talk to you about," Pilar says. "A little background first though."

She launches into a detailed account of the influence the oil companies have had on land development and specifically on housing. I can't imagine what this has to do with the sale of my uncle's house. My thoughts have wandered off to an evening in the company of the delectable Ander Ibarra when Pilar says, " . . . and so the oil company and the sheep men are symbiotic—sheep keep the grass cut, which makes it easier to get to the oil."

"I'm sorry, I'm not following. What deal?"

"Union Oil proposes to buy your uncle's house at a very good price."

"Why would they want it?"

"Good corporate citizenship. Their plan is to donate the house to the town for a Basque Cultural Studies Center."

"You are kidding." I think about that for a minute. "Do I detect the handiwork of Pilar and Ander Ibarra in all of this?" I laugh.

"You do. Here's the deal. We will form a board of directors and take proposals for study projects. I would really like to see someone come in and take oral histories from the families that have settled here."

"Celebrate plus educate equals perpetuate."

"Exactly right." Pilar looks delighted. "And I'd like you to serve on the board of directors."

"You aren't expecting me to live here, are you?"

"Of course not. You are a world traveler. This will be a piece of cake for you." Pilar forks a final bite of cake into her mouth, gulps the dregs of her coffee, and pushes herself away from the table. "Let's go; there's work to do."

On the way out, she says to Mayie, "Wonderful as always. Please put that on my tab."

She drives me to the edge of town and parks the car in front of a nondescript structure, the value of which must be in the land it sits on, adjacent to town.

"What's this?" We get out of the car and stand for awhile on the cracked sidewalk in front of an old house with peeling paint. A train moans in the distance. "I thought my uncle lived in a retirement community on some forested property out of town."

Pilar explains that this is the first of many houses my mother's uncle bought when his fortunes turned. This one he kept as an investment. Apparently, real-estate development is in the blood.

"We'll need to raise money to do some renovation, hire a director, and start some programs," Pilar says. "The house is small, but it will be perfect for our purpose, at least to start with. What do you think?"

"I'm on board."

"And your mother, what will she think?"

"I think she will be fine with this idea."

After I check into a motel and freshen up, Pilar and Andy pick me up and we head over to the Noriega Hotel. The Noriega is an *ostatu*, a Basque community center of sorts, located across the street from the Southern Pacific railroad tracks for the convenience of the men who drift into town looking for work. They rent rooms upstairs and eat their meals downstairs at a long table in a dining area next to the bar. Andy is surprised that I recognize the towering jai alai court that runs the full length of the hotel. I tell him about Elazar.

"You have a famous relative," Andy says. "I'm impressed! Some lively games happen here too. We'll be sure and get you out to one soon."

I flush at the thought of sitting close to Andy on the bleachers. I breathe him in, sun-bleached cotton, tanned leather, sweet hay, and desert sage. I have a strong urge to draw my hand across the plank of his shoulder, to tease my fingers through the black hair curling on his warm brown neck just above his shirt collar. Forcing my gaze to the rows of bottles shelved behind the bartender, I follow Andy and his sister over to the padded stools in the cocktail lounge where we find a perch among the chatty patrons. Eavesdropping on their conversations, I gather these are Basque people and other immigrants, Portuguese and Armenians, who live in the surrounding neighborhoods. The bartender makes a graceful swoop at the neck of an unidentified bottle of red wine and drops it in front of us with two glasses, nodding at Andy who lifts two fingers. He's a whiskey man.

Andy is a storyteller. His stories are very funny, and the hours pass quickly. I thought only people in Europe had this much fun in a roadhouse. I never expected to find such convivial company in Bakersfield.

Toward the end of the evening our conversation turns again to work we have ahead of us. I suggest that we call the proposed center the Iban and Alonso Moraga Cultural Studies Center. My companions applaud this idea and suggest a grand opening to coordinate with the annual picnic. We leave Noriega's around midnight.

I sleep late in the morning, but before I head out of town, I meet with Pilar to go over the details of the sale. We arrive at a plan to deal with the paperwork, agreeing that Andy will represent me in the sale.

"Can you come back in a few weeks to sign some legal documents?"

I promise I will. Walking back to the car, I put my hand in my coat pocket to fish out my keys and feel something else, a match cover or a coaster? I reach back into my pocket and retrieve a business card. ANDER IBARRA, ESQ. is embossed on the front. On the back, I see a scribble of words. I WILL BE IN SAN FRANCISCO NEXT WEEK. MAY I CALL YOU? ANDY.There is a phone number written in large and legible numerals.

Do I need another tall, dark, and handsome man in my life?

GREEN TIMES

*L*ife is slow here. It has taken me awhile to get used to that. Carmel is all art and no industry. I'm losing the sun now and feeling the chill in my bones. I bundle up in my bulky knit sweater and sit a bit longer on a bench looking out at the ocean, watching the dogs play with their people and sport with each other. The setting sun sparkles in the sea foam like diamonds, offering light but no warmth. The chill pulls tears from the corners of my eyes. I should have stopped at the bakery for a dose of coffee-and-pastry warmth.

The twisted trees in the distance have waltzed with the wind for centuries and they bear the scars. The raw beauty, the tango of wood and wind, compels me to reach for my camera one last time. I spend the waning light photographing the adagio effect of the wind on its partner. Then I pack up my camera, offer the backs of my icy fingers to a pooch that is trotting around collecting smells, and trudge back up the hill to town.

I've been here four months. Marianne was around at first. We scouted locations for the new art co-op, met with artists, and decided which ones would make the magic work. A co-op needs the right mix of media and artists who bring paying customers with them.

Dick and Marianne own a beach retreat on 17-Mile Drive. Her contacts are limitless, a testimony to her generous spirit. Of course she offered me lodging at the beach house, but I was determined to get a place of my own. I found a charming unit in a duplex a few blocks off Ocean Avenue and located a garage to rent for the Bel Air. I don't drive my car much because I can walk to the co-op from my apartment.

My neighborhood delivers what spring seed catalogs only promise—a riot of color. Carmel is a crazy quilt of gardens and houses that look like they were designed by gnomes. It lives a double life as a peaceful village and a growing tourist attraction. The mediator is the expansive Pacific Ocean, whose steady rumble sedates people into behaving well. I run the co-op, take photography classes from Wynn Bullock in Monterey and work on my collages in the co-op studio.

On days that I'm lucky enough to have a volunteer to relieve me in the co-op gift shop, I visit other galleries in town. After work, I walk down Scenic Road to clear my head and then grab a meal from one of my favorite cafés. I relish solitude after a full day talking shop with other storekeepers, discussing the state of art with visiting and resident artists, and answering questions about investment value from collectors.

My days are ordinary. Father Mike would say I'm in my green period—the time when the soul lies dormant, taking nutrition from stored reserves in preparation for another flowering. My companion these days is a treasured volume of *The Imitation of*

Christ. In Thomas A. Kempis's masterful meditation, I receive basic instructions in my new faith. I feel a Presence that plays host to the nameless emotions that spring free from some dark pool in my soul. Is it given to me, then, to name these creatures and put them to good use?

Roger calls once a week. We talk about our work and make plans to see each other. Our plans usually fall through because I can't find someone to babysit the co-op or he has to respond to a crisis at work. I think we both miss the easy familiarity of shared turf. We're not kids in thrall to romantic adventure; we're adults with an intimate need for the mundane. That sort of housekeeping doesn't appear to be in the immediate future.

Valerie is incredibly busy these days. I hear from her when she needs to give me an update on her little real-estate empire. As I anticipated, the Los Altos neighbors are not happy with the plan to let the lot sit empty until its new owner has time to think about what she really wants to do. Valerie has not been guarded enough about her plans and the neighborhood is ablaze with speculation. Rumors that Valerie is planning to build a group home for artists and writers or a safe house for fellow travelers have reached me through Laura.

"A single woman working on a doctorate who owns a prime piece of real estate in pristine Los Altos is highly suspect." Laura laughs. "The next-door neighbors are researching building codes and zoning laws."

"I imagine cease-and-desist warrants will add years to Valerie's plans. I'm just glad there is nothing left there to burn down," I say.

I miss Valerie. She pulls me into the concerns of her generation in ways that keep my perspective young. The Carmel population is an aging one.

This evening the sun is going down over the Pacific when I return to the co-op to make after-hours phone calls. I'm hoping to catch the painter I've hired and confirm that he will be in on Monday to prime a wall for a new exhibit. I set the burglar alarm, lock up and pop next door to pick up Chinese takeout. Walking home, the fragrance of chicken chow mien escapes the cardboard carton and genie-dances up my nose clear through my sinuses and springs to full flavor on my tongue. I pull my flashlight out of my pocket and begin to walk faster.

When it gets dark here, we rely on light from windows to guide us home. Street lights lack charm apparently, so they are banned. The local hospital emergency room does quite a business among tourists and locals alike who trip on tree roots and smack the pavement with such regularity that a column in the local newspaper is devoted to listing the injuries.

As I turn my key in the door of my duplex, it strikes me that my life is not fundamentally different than it would have been if I had stayed in Los Altos, except that the people I let into my life—Roger, Laura and Father Mike—graze in other pastures now. The change of scene is energizing, but my habits haven't changed. Is that comforting or depressing?

I heat water for the jasmine tea bag tucked into my take home and sit down at the kitchen table by the window to eat my dinner. It's a déjà vu moment, taking me back to when I would sit in the Los Altos house and stare out at my garden, ticking through all the tasks involved in preparing the soil for the next season. Leora's acerbic voice rings in my head clear as a bell—*What are you waiting for? An invitation?* What am I waiting for? I'm waiting for something.

❧ Dolores ❧

28

HEZITU

*V*alerie has said little about the property in Bakersfield except that an oil company bought the house
in town and the house in the hills is still for sale. She
assures me she will have a check for me soon. That
sale seems to require that she spend a lot of time in
Bakersfield. I can't see how she keeps up with her
studies, but she is almost twenty-seven, not seven-
teen. How she manages her schedule is her business.
She called last night to tell me she is driving over to
"share some exciting news." Those were her words,
and I turn them over in my head while I play with the
lighting on the new collection of paintings Marianne
acquired from the Jo Mora estate.

Exciting news could be anything—she got married and forgot to tell me and now she's expecting
my first grandchild; she's changed her field of study
to agricultural management and intends to annoy
the Los Altos neighbors by planting an experimental
community garden; she's adopted a cat.

Marianne sweeps through the door and inter-
rupts my reverie. Her Carmel persona is slightly

different from her Los Altos one, like the difference between shepherd's bread and San Francisco sourdough. She's saltier. Maybe I just know her better now.

"Dee! What an eye you have for lighting a Mora. The ocher tones? They pop in that light!" Like a tide that pulls silt off a glossy shell, Marianne polishes my better self and I glow. At that moment, Leora appears from some nether recess of my mind. She joins the party, sparkles here for a moment and then dissipates, leaving me with a bitter afterthought. Why could she not do what Marianne does with such graceful ease—make me feel good about myself? Deep in a sea cave in my heart, I hear the answer: despite her bravado, despite all her capability, Leora did not think of herself as a good person.

Marianne doesn't notice that my mind has left the building for awhile. She is lost in the exhibit. We reenter present time and review the promotional material. Then she lights out to meet her husband for dinner. I lock up and head home with some food I picked up at the corner deli.

When I round the corner, my old Chevy is parked on the street. Valerie found the key I left for her under the doormat because the lights are on in the front room and she is lounging in my armchair. I slow down and stand just out of sight, looking at the cozy domestic scene that plays out before me. A very handsome young man enters my living room from the kitchen with a bottle of wine and a tray of glasses.

My front door is slightly ajar. "Hey, Valerie, you made it," I say, so that I won't startle anyone as I push open the door.

Valerie rises from her chair and circles her hands around the young man's upper arm. "We got an early start to avoid the traffic; we've been here for awhile." A kitten is playing on the floor. A new man . . . and a cat?

"Mom, I want you to meet my friend Andy Ibarra."

Friend indeed. She is glowing.

"Andy, this is my mom, Dolores Moraga Carter." I've never heard my name put together that way. I set my bags down on the table and extend a hand.

"I'm Dee." Andy grabs my hand and gives it a good shake. "And who is this?"

I look down at a ball of white fluff that has flipped over on its back and is batting at my ankle. I bend down and scoop up a fat puffball that blinks at me with enormous blue eyes.

"That is Puffy, my new kitty," she says, puffing up a bit herself.

I can't imagine how she will fit a cat into her life.

Anyway, I'm more interested in where Andy fits. "Ibarra," I say. "Would you be . . . "

"Pilar's brother."

Cozy. That triggers another thought.

"Valerie, you should have let me know you were bringing a friend. I picked up some salads from the deli, but I can put them in the fridge and we can go out to eat. Would you like that?"

Then I address the young man. "Andy, I would love to offer to put you up for the night, but I only have one bedroom and a sleeper sofa for Valerie."

He puts up a hand. "Oh, no need, Mrs. Carter, I have a room at La Playa. I have plans to meet a friend tomorrow to play golf at Pebble Beach."

I discreetly raise an eyebrow at Valerie, who purses her lips into an enigmatic smile.

"Well that's fine, then. Let me take you to dinner at Paolina's. I think we still have time to catch the early-bird special. Is that okay?" I'm not about to try to impress a young man who apparently can afford to play golf at Pebble Beach.

"Valerie, will the kitten be all right here while we go out?" I've never had a cat, so I don't know.

"I'll settle Puffy in the kitchen with her kibble, water, and a litter box. I'll close the door so she won't wander. She'll be fine."

"Good," I manage to say, right after I recover from an attack of sneezing.

Dinner is pleasant. While Valerie is quick to establish Andy's credentials as an attorney, the young man himself is self-effacing. He has the easy manner of one who is either to the manor born or one who has been carefully schooled in egalitarian charm. I imagine he is a very good lawyer. Their company is enjoyable, but I don't learn much about the purpose of their visit. Is more news coming?

Valerie drives Andy to La Playa. She's gone a couple of hours. I make up her bed, play with the puffball for awhile, and then go to bed. I forget to close the kitten up in the kitchen. It's not long before I feel a tug on the bedspread as the kitten shimmies her way to the top of the bed Tarzan-style. She settles herself underneath my chin. My eyes start to water, but I enjoy her soft purr and the pressure of her warm belly pressing against my ear. *Ha, maybe what I've really needed all these years was a cat!* I sneeze and fall asleep.

The next morning my eyes are puffy and red. I banish the offender from my bedroom and take a shower to wash off her allergy-inducing dander. Valerie is apologetic. I suggest we go out for breakfast. I need air.

"So what's the exciting news?"

We each order juice, coffee, and Belgian waffles. She talks a little about our real-estate holdings, the role Pilar and Andy have played in brokering the sales, and finally she gets to the point. Iban's house near the railroad tracks is going to become some sort of Basque Center, named in honor of Iban and Alonso. Valerie will play some kind of continuing role in administering the Center.

"I knew you were interested in Spain. I had no idea you were interested in the Basque community in Bakersfield."

She sits up a little straighter in the booth. "I'm interested in our family history. And I have an opportunity to be involved with a project that educates children on their heritage and helps people maintain family connections." Her chin takes on an air of determination. "That is, if they choose to."

She rests her shoulders against the red padded booth, ignoring the head-banging three-year-old on the other side, and interlaces her fingers, resting them on the table in front of her plate. There's a buzzing in my head like an angry bee that has just been swatted. Before I can control my response, my hand slaps down hard on the table. This silences the head-banger and causes Valerie to drop her hands into her lap and fight to keep the tears that have jumped into her eyes from spilling over.

"Look, Valerie, I'm not stupid. It hasn't been too hard to figure out that you somehow unearthed the story on your own. You know that Alaya is still alive in

Spain. I'm guessing that you may have even met her on your last visit."

Valerie's face turns a color that matches the strawberry syrup chilling in the wells of her soggy waffles.

I continue. "That's your business. I don't need to hear about it."

We square off in silence for a full minute. She rolls her hand around an orange she filched from the fruit basket, and for a moment I fear she might pick it up and fling it at me. Instead, she grows thoughtful.

She shakes her head. "The two of you are identical in every way I can think of, but most of all in stubbornness. Each of you leaves it to the other to make the first move, and you both try to put me in the middle. But here is how it's going to be. Next month, the Iban and Alonso Moraga Center for Basque Cultural Studies will have its grand opening. Both you and Alaya will receive a formal invitation to be a part of celebrating the lives of your father and your uncle. Come or don't come, it's your choice." Then she shoves a huge bite of waffle into her mouth. "I need to get back and check on Puffy."

❧ Dolores ☙

29

BETIKOTU

My invitation arrives on May 1, 1955. It is an elaborate summons describing a two-day event that includes the annual picnic at the Basque Club, a dinner at the Wool Growers Café to install the Center's new board of directors, and a ribbon-cutting ceremony to officially open the Center. Dinner tickets and a voucher for a two- night stay at the El Tejon Hotel are tucked inside, along with a personal note from Pilar expressing her hope that I will attend. I notice that Alaya Moraga and Dolores Moraga Carter are listed as guests of honor. Also listed are Elazar Palacios and Domeka and Danel Palacios. Valerie and I have had a few tense conversations over the last few months so I know this is Alaya's family. I surmise it's a cultural norm for the woman who inherits the family home to keep the family name.

Fittingly, these events are to take place over Memorial Day weekend. That's when I'd planned to visit Roger in New York, so there's my excuse.

When he calls, I tell all this to Roger.

"Dee, don't be silly. Of course we should reschedule New York and you should go to the ceremony."

"What will I do if Alaya comes?"

"Shake her hand and say 'Nice to meet you'? Give her a hug and say 'It's about time'? You'll think of something to say. Don't worry about that."

"What if she doesn't come?"

"Then you won't have lost anything you didn't lose a long time ago."

I mull over his words.

"Dee, would you like me to come out and go with you?"

"No, Roger, I need to do this by myself. What I'd like is if you would reschedule my visit to New York. However this plays out, I'm going to need a good cry. And you've got the shoulder I want to cry on."

"Okay then, you got it. I'll go buy a really absorbent shirt."

Next, I think about calling Father Mike or driving to Los Altos to see him. I don't do it though. Instead, I sit on my bench at Carmel River State Beach and talk to God. I am just learning to pray. Instead of asking questions, I pour out my sadness and frustration, anger and disappointment. These emotions are like a deep well to which I add my fear of being hurt and disappointed. I add a little hope that things might turn out well for everyone. Then I go home, seal and stamp my acceptance, and mail it.

Valerie has been in Bakersfield for two weeks getting ready for the big day. How does she maintain her standing at Stanford? Where does she stay when she's in Bakersfield? I imagine the possibilities. One attribute I have discovered that I hold in common with my mother is how important it is for a single woman to maintain a good reputation, but Valerie's generation seems unconcerned with propriety. I walk a tightrope in my relationship with my adult daughter that stretches between openness and circumspection. I won't ask. I just pray she isn't doing anything that would jeopardize her future happiness.

When I pull the Bel Air into the hotel parking lot, I'm so nervous that I'm shaking. I haul a big suitcase out of the trunk of my car. I couldn't decide between three different outfits for the ceremony, so I brought them all. I check in at the desk and go up to my room. On the desk by the phone is a note from Valerie that directs me to call her the minute I get in. She's in room 403.

Valerie picks up the phone on the first ring. "Mom," she says in a practiced, mature, calm voice. "Aunt Alaya is here."

"Here? Here in Bakersfield? Here in the hotel?"

"Yes, she's here in the hotel. She's come with her husband and the twins. What do you want, Mom? Do you want to meet her alone or with her family?"

"What does she want?"

"I think we'll get the two of you together first."

Five minutes later Valerie knocks on my door. I'm still wearing the slacks and blouse I drove here in, but I've combed my hair and refreshed my makeup. If I look disheveled, Valerie doesn't comment. She takes my hand and we walk down the hallway, down the stairs, through the lobby, and through smoked-glass doors into a small parlor. I try to decide where to stand. I go to the window that faces the door and half sit on the window ledge, crossing my legs at the ankle and jiggling a foot. Valerie is making small talk, asking me about the drive, burbling on about the preparations for the ceremony.

Two shadows appear at the door, and Valerie falls quiet. The door squeaks open and Pilar enters the room with Alaya in tow. Then Pilar signals Valerie, and they both leave.

An electric jolt spins through my body as I look over at a trimmer version of myself standing elegant and still before me. Dressed in a white shawl-collared blouse tucked into a black pencil skirt, my sister searches my face with familiar dark chocolate eyes and I see Leora's ironic smile begin to form on her lips. Funny, I never see anything of Leora when I look at myself in the mirror, but I see Leora written all over Alaya. I am being presented with a rare opportunity.

Character is bred over generations. In my profound ignorance of what caused our mother to disconnect from intimate relationships and forge a solitary life, I never thought about what restless spirit drove her. Alaya and I are two sides of a coin—where she is peaceful I am restless, and those qualities both come from our mother. We both missed the opportunity to pry family history out of Leora, but now we have a chance to talk to each other, to piece together some of this puzzle that is our family.

These thoughts occur to me in the flash it takes me to push myself up from the window ledge and move toward her. We burst into tears and fall on each other—the years fade and it's as if we were toddlers making up after a fuss, not forty-seven-year-old strangers. We cling and sob and laugh and try to talk. We sit side by side on a settee in a corner of the room, hold hands, and marvel at how we mirror each other.

"We are mirror twins," Alaya says. "Papito told me that. That means we separated late in the womb. You are left-handed?"

"Yes."

"I'm right-handed."

This twin thing is a whole new universe.

We agree that there will be time to share our experiences, to piece together our parents' story, to fill in the missing years. I tell her that I look forward to meeting her husband and my nephews. I open her hand and place a gift in it, the sheep bell with the inscription *Ardi galdua atzeman daiteke, aldi galdua berriz ez.* She reads it in the old language. Then she translates for me: *Lost sheep may be recovered. Lost time cannot.*

We can't restore the past, but over time we can reconfigure the family. This weekend we will stand together and celebrate that we are Moragas, that we are Basque, and that we have a legacy to perpetuate.

EPILOGUE

*I*n June, I meet Roger at the Waldorf Astoria in New York City. He's made dinner reservations at Tavern on the Green. We have tickets to see Cole Porter's *Silk Stockings* and plans to visit as many art galleries as our feet will carry us through. I have another thought as well.

"Roger? Do you happen to know where the Greek part of New York City is?"

ACKNOWLEDGMENTS

Grateful thanks to the Center for Basque Studies, University of Reno and to Daniel Montero, for publishing *The Sheep Walker's Daughter* as a Basque Original. I also want to thank the people who encouraged me, The Sonora Writers Group; NaNoWriMo; Seth Harwood, author and teacher; David Hough, editor; my team at Writer's Relief, and Lynellen Perry. Many thanks to family and friends who gave feedback on my early efforts, Peggy Andrews, Arnette Cratty, Etty Garber, Virginia Gustafson, Calder Lowe, Julie McVicker, Beth Palmer, Jeanie Pierce, April Trabucco and Cheryl von Drehle, and to the women in my Bible Study for their prayers. Finally, special thanks to Joel Avey, my aviation expert and loving husband who let me turn our lives upside down to become an author.

Author's Note

Writing *The Sheep Walker's Daughter* was my introduction to the Basque culture. Growing up in the post-WWII multicultural San Francisco Bay Area, I came to appreciate how a knowledge of ethnic and cultural heritage enriches people and communities. When it came time to choose a heritage for the Moraga family, I decided to choose a culture that many people know little about. Dee's adventure of discovery became my own. That there is a vibrant Basque community in Bakersfield, CA, a half-day drive from my home, gave me an opportunity to visit the setting for my book. Not only could I view the train tracks the Basque sheepherders would have crossed to the Noriega Hotel where they boarded, I could taste the food they ate and talk to a few men who had herded sheep before moving on to other endeavors. In researching the immigrant experience of the Basques I discovered a resilience, resourcefulness, and enterprising spirit that served my story well. I also found a vegetable soup recipe that is a keeper!

ABOUT THE AUTHOR

Sydney Avey writes about the human experience in an uncertain world. She is the author of three historical fiction novels, *The Sheep Walker's Daughter*, *The Lyre and the Lambs*, and *The Trials of Nellie Belle*. Her work has appeared in *Foliate Oak*, *Forge*, *American Athenaeum*, *Unstrung*, *Blue Guitar Magazine*, *Ruminate*, and *MTL Magazine*. She has studied at the Iowa Summer Writing Festival. Sydney and her airplane enthusiast husband divide their time between the Sierra Nevada foothills of Yosemite, California, and the Sonoran Desert in Arizona.

Find Sydney online:

SydneyAvey@Gmail.com
www.SydneyAvey.com
Facebook.com/YosemiteSyd
Pinterest.com/yosemitesyd/
Twitter: @SydneyAvey

Made in the USA
San Bernardino, CA
02 October 2017